SECRET OF THE VAMPIRE

DEATHLESS NIGHT-INTO THE DARK #2

L.E. WILSON

EVERBLOOD
PUBLISHING

ALSO BY L.E. WILSON

Deathless Night Series (The Vampires)

A Vampire Bewitched

A Vampire's Vengeance

A Vampire Possessed

A Vampire Betrayed

A Vampire's Submission

A Vampire's Choice

Deathless Night-Into the Dark Series (The Vampires)

Night of the Vampire

Secret of the Vampire

Forsworn by the Vampire

The Kincaid Werewolves (The Werewolves)

Lone Wolf's Claim

A Wolf's Honor

The Alpha's Redemption

A Wolf's Promise

A Wolf's Treasure

The Alpha's Surrender

Southern Dragons (Dragon Shifters & Vampires)

Dance for the Dragon

Burn for the Dragon

Snow Ridge Shifters (Novellas)

A Second Chance on Snow Ridge

A Fake Fiancé on Snow Ridge

Copyright © 2021 by Everblood Publishing, LLC

All rights reserved. No part of this publication may be reproduced, distributed, or transmitted in any form or by any means, including photocopying, recording, or other electronic or mechanical methods, without the prior written permission of the publisher, except in the case of brief quotations embodied in critical reviews and certain other noncommercial uses permitted by copyright law. For permission requests, email the publisher, addressed "Attention: Permissions Coordinator," at the address below.

All characters and events in this book are fictitious. Any resemblance to actual persons – living or dead – is purely coincidental.

le@lewilsonauthor.com

ISBN:978-1-945499-36-4

Print Edition

Publication Date: February 18, 2021

Developmental Editor: Sara Lunsford @ Book Frosting

Copy Editor: Jinxie Gervasio @ jinxiesworld.com

Cover Design by Coffee and Characters

NOTE FROM THE AUTHOR

I mentioned this in book 1, but I thought it was worth repeating...

If you are new to my books, there are a few things you need to know about this series to avoid any confusion.

The "Deathless Night-Into the Dark" series is an *extension* of the original "Deathless Night" series, picking up the storyline of The Moss Witches that was started in the original series. And, the characters from Deathless Night will be making appearances throughout this series, starting right here in Secret of the Vampire.

I'm thrilled to be with these characters again, and I hope you are, too!

Happy reading, and I hope you enjoy Alex and Kenya's story!

1

KENYA

Something slick and evil crawled over my skin, like a thousand tiny spiders slipping beneath my clothes, making me shudder in the damp night air.

It was menacing.

Angry.

Someone was watching, and they wanted something from me. Something I instinctively knew I wouldn't give up willingly. I could feel their intentions all the way down to my bones.

My gums burned as my fangs shot down into my mouth, every muscle in my body tense, ready to strike. To kill if I had to.

Though I truly wished I wouldn't have to.

Somehow, I kept a grip on my keys, even though my hand was shaking like crazy, pretending I was having trouble with the lock to the door of the club. Pushing my glasses up with one finger, I glanced discreetly to my left.

Bourbon Street was in full-on holiday mode; the balconies and street poles wrapped in Christmas lights, with sprigs of evergreens here and there to break it up. Even the usual stench that seeped through the ground wasn't so bad, thanks to the cooler air.

It was Thursday night, and the crowd at The Purple Fang—our vampire-owned, male strip club where I tended bar and kept the books—had been sparse. Killian had decided to close it down early so he could go home to his Lizzy, and the rest of the coven could find their amusements elsewhere in The Quarter. I'd stayed behind alone so as not to impede on anyone's fun. I was still trying to catch up on some reports that I'd missed when I was dying.

Yes, dying. Unheard of for a vampire, I know.

It's a long story, but not really surprising if you knew me at all.

At first, I saw nothing unusual. A few groups of die-hards who didn't want the party to end even though the street cleaners and trash trucks were starting to rumble through the streets, a homeless person, strippers making their way home or heading to a late-night party.

I twisted the keys in the lock and pulled them out, backing up a few steps as I dropped them into my bag with my laptop. Lifting my chin, I scented the air, searching for whatever it was that was making me so uneasy. I smelled alcohol, fresh vomit, body odor, trash, sewage, and the warm blood of the few humans still on the street. Keeping my expression impassive, I turned and started to walk away. Our residence was only a few blocks from here. I just needed to make it to the house. And hopefully, the guys would be home by now.

Don't get me wrong, I wasn't helpless. Far from it. But ever since my last brush with magic, I've been a little on the jumpy side, and the devilry I felt hovering in the air tonight felt way too familiar. It was unnerving to say the least.

Terrifying was more like it.

The hair lifted on the back of my bare neck before I could take more than a few steps, and I would swear to anyone who asked I felt hot breaths on my skin beneath my hairline. Spinning around, I flashed my fangs with a hiss...

But there was no one there.

I adjusted my glasses, checking again. Breathing hard, my eyes darted up and down the darkened street, my nerves on edge, and when my cell phone buzzed in the front pocket of my black slacks, I barely caught myself before I shrieked like a teenager in a bad horror movie.

I hated horror movies.

Especially ones with stupid teenage girls.

With a shaking hand, I tugged my phone out and answered the call, pushing up my glasses with my free hand as I glanced over my shoulder. My one complaint about becoming a vampire was that, strangely enough, it hadn't corrected my vision. "Hello?"

"Get back inside the club and lock the doors. Right now," the voice on the other end growled. "I'm on my way."

"Alex?"

"Just do what I fucking say, Kenya."

I opened my mouth to tell him...something smart and female empowered, but he'd already hung up. After a moment's hesitation, I dug the keys back out of my bag and got my ass back inside. Someone, or some*thing,* was out there, and it did not want me to make it home. So, I swallowed my initial reaction to being ordered around and did what Alex told me to do.

He *had* helped me once, after all. I had no reason to believe he wouldn't do so again.

At least, I didn't think I had any reason to believe that. He was a bit...intense.

If any humans had been paying attention, they would've seen a woman standing on the sidewalk looking scared and confused one second and gone the next. But I had no time to worry about that. Luckily, anyone still stumbling around Bourbon Street at this time of night either wouldn't notice or wouldn't remember. They would probably just blink rapidly a few times and tell their friends how good the Hurricanes at Pat O'Brien's were.

Plus, I had bigger things to worry about right now.

I locked the door and backed up toward the bar, stashing my bag underneath. Taking off my coat, I folded it over my arm and tucked it on the shelf beside it. Then I kicked off my heels and stretched my bare feet. I needed my movements to be unhampered. Whatever was out there, common sense told me a locked door wasn't going to keep it out, and I wasn't about to just sit around and wait for Alex to get here and "save" me.

Opening the screen on my cell, I started to tap out a quick text to Killian, the master vampire of my coven and head of the only family I'd ever known. But then I paused. Alex was on his way, and if Killian caught him here without his permission there would be hell to pay. And if I had to choose a champion, I'd rather have a scary warlock on my side to fight dark magic.

Deleting the message, I slid my phone into my bag where it wouldn't get damaged. I could always call Killian after the fact to walk me home.

If I made it out of here.

The club was dark except for a light over the bar, and I moved into the shadows near the door. My pants and blouse were both black, and with my dark skin and hair, it would hopefully give me a chance to surprise them.

I needed one second to get the upper hand.

Just one.

Time ticked silently by, and although I felt that whoever or whatever was stalking me was still outside, it made no move to try to get into the club. Yet I could feel how restless it was becoming, like vibrations in the air. Could almost see it pacing the sidewalk just outside.

I swallowed down my anxiety and tried to calm my heart, which was doing its best to break through the cage of my breastbone. My glasses slid slowly down my nose, but I didn't dare move.

It had been stupid of me to stay here alone, especially after I'd promised Alex I wouldn't when he'd checked on me after my illness. But nothing had happened for weeks, and we had all started to relax back into our normal lives. Even Killian, the ever-watchful master vampire, had only given me a thoughtful glance when I'd told him I was going to stay late to catch up on things. Then he'd given me a nod and told me not to get caught by the sun before he'd hurried home to his mate.

As I waited, my mind wandered back to the night Alex had saved my life. Killian had hidden me at the swamp house after I'd fallen ill, and no one had known what was happening. But I did. I was dying, rotting from the inside out, something unheard of for one of my species. Vampires died by things like beheadings or sunlight, not from a horrible case of the flu.

But what I'd had was much worse than a common virus. It was a curse. And not a normal curse. With no other options, Killian had called in the witches we shared the city of New Orleans with. But even they hadn't known where it had come from or who had placed it. Lucky for me, Alex had stepped up completely on a whim and tried to help. He'd torn it out of me with his bare hands.

Well, it was magic, but it sure as hell had *felt* like his bare hands had reached inside of me to rip it out.

Quite a different feeling from the way he'd touched me the next time I'd seen him, right here at the club at closing time, his large palm flat against my chest, radiating heat through my body as he searched for any remaining signs of the curse.

A noise outside the door brought me back to the here and now with a vengeance. I hissed, my fangs bared and my hands up, fingers curled into lethal claws. Whoever was coming after me, I wasn't going down without one hell of a fight.

The scent of blood assaulted my senses. My own. Vaguely, I noticed the tip of my left middle finger was bleeding. I must've nicked it on something coming back into the club.

"Kenya! Let me in."

It was Alex. Even if I hadn't recognized his voice, I would've known it was him by the way my body immediately went on alert, ready for a different kind of battle.

One that involved who was going to be on top.

"Kenya!"

Shaking off the untoward thought, I unlocked the door and stepped back out of the way of the door. Alex hurried inside, closing and locking it behind him.

He was dressed in jeans and his dark green coat, much as he was the last time I'd seen him. I barely came to the top of his shoulder without my heels on. And with his broad shoulders, dark hair, intense golden eyes, and olive-toned skin...

He took my breath away.

And gods, he smelled better than any human I'd ever fed on. It was completely distracting.

However, it didn't matter if I found him attractive. Alex was a warlock. I was a vampire. Two lines that weren't allowed to cross.

"What are you doing here? And how did you get my number?" I asked him.

Taking my face between his palms, his golden eyes held mine for a few seconds before he released me and stepped back, raking his eyes up and down my body. Then he grabbed my shoulders, spearing me with his gaze. "Are you okay?"

I nodded. "Yes, I'm fine."

As though he'd only just realized what he was doing, he dropped his hands and took a step back. But his eyes never left me.

I wrapped my arms around my waist, his rejection making me feel cold. Then I scolded myself. The hot warlock was not what I needed to be focusing on right now. "Alex, who's out there?"

He shook his head. "I don't know. But they can't get in here."

"How do you know that?"

He smiled, but it wasn't a pleasant smile. More a twist of his mouth that was somewhat rebellious and utterly sexy. "I put a ward around the building the night I came here to check on you. I came back after you'd left."

"You did?"

"I did."

It didn't surprise me that no one had noticed. The Quarter was full of magic, both light and dark, and that didn't even take into account all of the voodoo floating around. It would take something completely different—like the thing hunting me—for anyone to pause and take notice.

Concern for his safety quickly replaced any misguided feelings of inadequacy I was feeling. "Alex, magic without permission is forbidden in our territory."

He narrowed his eyes at me, surprised by my response. "You're angry?"

"Would it matter to you if I was?"

Slowly, he shook his head. "No. I still would've taken the risk to protect you."

I stared at him, unsure of what to say. Did he feel some sort of responsibility for me now that he had cured me? Or was there some other reason he was so invested? And what if it wasn't a good reason? Alex was the only member of the witch coven who'd known how to release me from the curse. And if I remembered correctly, even Judy—the High Priestess *and* his aunt—had been surprised.

Of course, I'd been on death's door at the time. Maybe my mind was playing tricks on me.

A movement outside the tinted glass drew my attention and my heart stopped as my head whipped around, but it was just a group of people walking by.

I turned back to Alex. For now, he was all I had. And I wasn't ready to turn on him. Not just yet. "What do we do now? How do we get out of here?"

His eyes travelled over my face again, then dropped briefly to my chest before meeting my stare directly. He gently adjusted my glasses, then dropped his arms back down to his sides. "We don't, Kenya. We're going to have to stay here until morning."

"But I can't wait until morning. The sun—"

"Will burn you to ash. I know."

I didn't say anything else, just raised one eyebrow, a silent question asking him, *then how the hell am I supposed to get home?* I didn't like this.

Running a hand through his short, dark hair, he began to pace back and forth in front of me, his brows furrowed in thought.

A sudden thought occurred to me. "Does the High Priestess know you're here? Did you tell her you were coming?"

His steps slowed, but only for a moment before picking up speed again. His eyes searched out mine and he gave a quick shake of his head before dropping them back to the floor. "No. I had no time."

I made a decision. "Alex, you need to go. I appreciate you trying to help me, but you're taking too big of a risk." Plus, this entire situation was just making me extremely uncomfortable. I was a vampire, yes. But I wasn't a very good one. And Alex had magic strong enough to easily overpower me. I could practically see it coiling around him from here.

"I'm not leaving you here alone with..." He slashed a hand toward the front of the club when the right word didn't come to him. Closing his eyes, he stopped pacing and rubbed them with the thumb and forefinger of one hand. "I'm not leaving you alone, Kenya. Judy cannot stop me from protecting you."

"But why do you want to?" At his frown, I crossed my arms and cocked my head to the side in challenge, putting on a bravado I didn't feel. "I'm a vampire, Alex. I'm not yours to protect."

"And yet, I'm going to do it anyway." His voice was little more than a growl. A challenge. Then he sighed heavily. "Look, I don't know what that is out there, but I can feel it, Kenya."

"Of course, you can. It's magic. Even I can feel it and I'm not a witch."

He walked over to a stool at one of the high tables and climbed on, resting his elbows on the table. He stared at the tabletop for a long moment before he looked back up at me. "That's not what I'm talking about."

"What *are* you talking about?" I asked him.

"I mean, I can feel it. Inside of me. Magic to magic. Whatever is out there," he pointed toward the locked door, "some of it is also in me."

Restlessly, he got up from the table and walked over to the door near where I stood. There were no windows. No way to see outside. However, I didn't need to see out to know something was still out there.

And neither did he.

2

ALEX

I was obsessed.

Ever since the night I'd saved the vampire—Kenya—I haven't been able to think of anything else but her. Whether she was okay. Whether she was safe.

Whether she was thinking of me, too.

I'd seen her around before then, of course. In order to share this fine city, my coven and hers occasionally had to work out some rules. So, the High Priestess and their master vampire would meet up to pound out details of our pact or to be made aware of something that was going on that would affect all of us. But that was normally the extent of our involvement with each other. Otherwise, we pretty much stuck to our part of the city and the vampires, at least for now, were content to live and feed within the seventy-eight-square block radius of the most sinful part of New Orleans.

As long as they didn't terrorize the tourists and kept their victims alive and without any memories of their encounters with the blood suckers, we dealt with coexisting, with the agreement we would help one another if either of our covens was threatened.

So, of course, I'd seen the female vampire before, but only from a distance. I knew she was attractive in a sexy librarian kind of way, with her confident airs and her dark-rimmed glasses. I'd also overheard she was the one who ran the club the vampires owned, so I knew she was intelligent. And yeah, okay. I'd always had a thing for her. She was exactly my type of female.

However, until the night I'd saved her life, I'd never been close enough to see how smooth and perfect her skin was, even flushed with fever. Never knew how her brown eyes bared her soul to me. How sweet she smelled. How soft the texture of her hair was, or how her smile would stop my heart.

Even so, I knew I should put her out of my mind. She wasn't mine. Wasn't for me. The fact that I'd saved her life meant nothing.

But as the days passed, I'd found it harder and harder to stay away. I knew she must've lived, thanks to my coven's interference, or we would've heard something about it. We would've felt the other vampire's grief echoing through the city like shock waves from an atomic bomb. But we heard nothing. So, I knew she was alive.

Still, I couldn't get her out of my fucking head. And so, one night long after closing time, I took the risk and entered the vampire's territory alone so I could see for myself. She was still at the club, I felt it in my gut, and I was hoping I'd catch her alone.

Unsure of how she would react if I took it upon myself to just walk in, I waited across the street for her to come out. I didn't have to wait long, just a few minutes before she stepped outside and locked the door. She spotted me as she turned to leave, surprise flitting across her face for a brief moment before she quickly waved me over to her.

I'd only wanted to make sure I'd gotten all of the curse out of her and that she wasn't having any kind of after effects, or at least that's what I'd told myself. When I placed my hand on the center of her chest to run a magical scan, the instant spark between us seemed to shock her. But I wasn't surprised. I'd even tried to prepare myself for it. "Tried" being the key word there. There was a connection between us I'd never felt with any other woman. I'd always known it. And now it was even stronger.

Yet, even knowing she had fully recovered, even after placing a protection spell around the building where she spent her time at night and warning her not to be alone, I couldn't stop.

I took to prowling the perimeter of The Quarter like some sort of magical watchdog, watching over her from afar. "Listening" for anything out of the ordinary. Any kind of magic that wasn't familiar or didn't belong.

All I knew was that night we went to the swamp house and I'd reached inside of Kenya to pull out the ugliness that was killing her, something had shifted inside of me. I'm not sure what it was exactly, or why it had happened. Maybe because my magic had been inside of her...

No, it was more than that. *I* had been inside of her. All of me. That's what it had taken to save her. And like some kind of goddamned avenging angel, I'd felt her surround me with her light, protecting me from the darkness even as I ripped it from her weakened body. The darkness I should not have been able to save her from. The darkness that was much more familiar to me than not. The darkness I also sensed in my twin sister, Alice, although it wasn't as strong and she would never admit it. Not even to me.

As for me and Kenya...it was like our souls had fucking touched.

And somehow, I'd known that even though the curse was gone, it wasn't over. I'd felt something coming for weeks now. And the thought of whatever the hell that was returning for her terrified the fuck out of me. I couldn't lose her. Not when I'd only just found her.

So, I'd kept watch.

And tonight, my stubbornness had paid off. I was walking along the edge of The Quarter when I'd felt its presence, oozing with malevolence, but no viler than what was inside of me.

Pushing aside my terror, I'd closed my eyes, reached out, and found Kenya, alone on Bourbon Street. I didn't know who or what this was or why it was coming back for her, but the fucker would have to go through me first.

And here I was, coming to the vampire's club once more with no thought to my coven's anger or my own safety. I had to. I had no choice. This female vampire pulled me to her, even though I tried to resist, an erotic tug of war I had no defense against. I had to protect her.

"Alex? Do you know what it is? *Who* it is?"

Kenya's voice yanked me from my thoughts. I shook my head without looking at her. If I looked at her, I'd want to kiss her. And more. A sudden surge of desire had me gritting my teeth. Willing my pulse to slow, knowing she would hear it, I tried to get my mind back onto the threat at hand. "I have no idea," I admitted to her. "But I won't let it hurt you."

I felt her stare.

"Thank you," she told me softly.

Her voice was low. Sexy. Closing my eyes, I let it drift over me. My body far more aware of her than the danger outside.

"So, we just wait it out?"

"It can't get through my ward, or it would've done so by now," I assured her.

I felt her eyes on me again and knew what she would ask next. "What if it doesn't leave?"

That was a good question. Turning to her, I took her face in my hands, careful of her glasses. I'd never before heard of a vampire who had kept any kind of human deficiencies after turning until I'd met Kenya. But it was something I would ask about another time. "Nothing will happen to you. I swear it."

My thumb grazed her smooth cheek.

"Why are you here?" she asked abruptly.

Distracted by the softness of her skin, I didn't hear her question at first.

"Why, Alex? Why are you willing to risk yourself for me?" Her eyes sought and held mine.

"I don't know," I admitted quietly.

That seemed to surprise her, but then she composed herself. "I appreciate what you did tonight. I do. But there's no reason for you to be here."

Her meaning was clear. She was telling me she wasn't my problem. That whatever it was I felt toward her wasn't mutual.

But she was lying.

She must've seen the determination on my expression, for a second later, her chin rose in defiance.

We stood like that for a long time, searching for something within the other. Something we both desperately wanted but shouldn't take.

It was Kenya who broke the spell, stepping back out of my hold. "I should call Killian. Let him know what's going on. He's expecting me back at the house."

"If you call him, won't he come here?"

"If I don't call him, he'll definitely show up. He's very... protective of those he considers his."

White hot rage blurred my vision, unbidden and uncalled for. But I couldn't control it. Killian may be the one who created her, but Kenya wasn't his. Not any longer.

She was *mine*.

The thought startled me, and it was a moment before I realized Kenya was staring at me, a strange expression on her pretty face. Sometimes a vampire's heightened senses were a pain in the ass. I took a few deep breaths to calm myself, pretty damned surprised myself by the realization that had just slammed through me. Not so much a coherent thought as a feeling. An instinct. I shook it off. She wasn't mine. I just felt protective of her because I'd saved her life. "What are you going to tell him?"

Thankfully, she didn't question me about my reaction to what she'd said about Killian. Instead, she walked over to the bar, sexier and more natural in bare feet than she would be in the heels I just noticed kicked under a bar stool, her rounded ass holding my attention until she got behind the bar. Getting her phone from behind it, she propped her elbows on the wooden surface and stared down at the screen. "I don't know. But I have to tell him something. He's expecting me home," she repeated.

I wracked my brain. "Do you have a friend? Someone you'd hang out with?"

A smile teased the corners of her full lips. "No. I have my family. The guys," she clarified.

"And you all live together in that big house." Jealousy made my words come out harsher than I'd intended.

She looked at me over the rim of her glasses, the gape of her blouse giving me a peek of full breasts, and my cock swelled, the zipper of my jeans digging into me uncomfortably.

"It's safer for us that way."

A scene from the movie *The Lost Boys* popped into my head. The one where the kids went into the vampire cave to stake them and found them all hanging from the ceiling like bats.

"It's not like that," she told me with a roll of her eyes.

I narrowed my eyes. "Stay out of my head." I didn't mean to be so harsh, but there were things about me I wasn't ready for her to know. Not to mention what my cock was doing.

The smile fell from her face and she swallowed, her head falling forward as she looked down at her phone again. "Sorry. I didn't mean to. I just..." Taking a deep breath, she lifted her chin and met my eyes. "I'm sorry. I don't make it a habit to invade the personal thoughts of others. I...slipped."

I exhaled and gave her a nod. But just in case she "slipped" again, I raised my shields. It was stupid of me to forget they could do that. "Don't call Killian. I'll get you home safe before the sun comes up."

She paused, thumbs poised over the screen. She didn't seem to believe me. "Are you sure? What if whoever—or whatever—that is, comes after us?"

I looked down at the floor, opening myself up to the power on the other side of these walls. It was still there, hovering like a caged animal, but otherwise making no moves to test the ward I'd placed. "I don't think it will."

"It's not gone," she said.

"No," I confirmed. I was quickly learning a vampire's instincts were nothing to mess around with. She could feel threats as well as I could. Not the small nuances, I would imagine, but just that it was there. "No, it's not gone. But it's also not trying to get in. It's watching."

"Because of the ward around the club," she said, but her tone was unsure.

I shook my head. "No. It barely even tested it. Honestly, I think it was just surprised that it was there." I started to prowl back and forth on the other side of the bar, hands linked behind my back and my head down as I contemplated our situation and how I would go about keeping my word to Kenya if that...thing, or whatever it was...decided to camp out on the street until we were forced to leave.

And what if I was wrong? What if I took her from the safety of the club and it was waiting for us? Would I be able to fend it off?

Maybe I should call the rest of the coven. Or at least Angel. She knows how to keep her mouth shut, if I can manage to hunt her down in time. I would call Alice too, but unfortunately, I can't say the same for my sister. Her loyalty to the High Priestess comes before all else with her.

Even her own brother.

No. I was on my own in this. It was better this way. I'm the one who broke the rules and got involved with a vampire. I should be the only one to deal with the consequences of my actions.

Decision made, I joined Kenya at the bar. Putting my elbows on the smooth service, I leaned in toward her and kept my voice low in case it was listening. "We'll wait until right before sunrise. The city will be coming awake and more people will be out on the streets. I don't think it wants to be seen."

"How do you know?"

"I don't. Not really. It's just a feeling."

"You're betting our lives on a feeling?"

I smiled, trying to reassure her. "This thing doesn't know what it's fucking with."

"Or maybe *you* don't know what *you're* fucking with."

"Ye of such little faith," I teased.

My words didn't bring the smile back to her face as I'd hoped they would. Reaching across the bar, I covered one of her small hands with mine. "Besides, as you yourself said, Killian would kill me—piece by piece—if I allowed anything to happen to you. And then he would turn me just so he could kill me again."

"You would never allow him that close to you."

She had a point. "It would be harder to hold back five vampires. Especially if Judith gives me over to them."

Kenya looked down at her hand, still covered with mine, but made no move to remove it. "I find that hard to believe. She's your auntie."

"And she would happily sacrifice me to keep the peace between our two covens." I honestly didn't know if this was true or not, but if it would help me convince Kenya...

Her eyes clashed with mine and I caught a flash of her fangs before she remembered herself. My cock, which had just started to behave itself, perked up with renewed interest. Apparently, it wasn't afraid of a little danger. And I had no doubt I'd just caught a glimpse of a side to this vampire I would not want to meet alone on a darkened street.

Willing my sex to calm the fuck down, I watched her response. It was an interesting reaction, to say the least, from a vampire who had, just a few minutes before, implied she cared nothing about me as a man.

Stashing this little memory away for later, I focused on the problem at hand. "We'll leave just before dawn, but in plenty of time to get you to shelter before the sun rises." I tightened my fingers on hers. "You can trust me, Kenya."

For a moment, she just stared at me. "Looks like I'm gonna have to," she finally said. Then she pulled her hand from mine, stashed her cell back under the bar, and grabbed a bottle of expensive vodka from the shelf behind her. She poured two shots, sliding one over to me. "But if we're gonna die, we might as well go out in style."

I clinked my glass to hers and downed the shot. The alcohol burned, distracting me from the pretty bartender. But not nearly enough. "We're not going to die."

"But if I do, I'm haunting you and your family."

I smiled as she poured us another shot.

3

KENYA

Alex and I stood in front of the locked door of the club. I had my shoes on, my coat on, and my keys out, ready to lock it up behind us and run for our lives. The strap of my bag crossed my body so I wouldn't lose it if it came down to that. We had about 30 minutes to get me home and inside before the sun rose over the horizon, and I offered up a quick prayer that he was right and his plan would work.

Beside me, the warlock was strangely calm.

"Are you ready?" he asked.

"As ready as I'll ever be," I answered. It was a complete and utter lie. I wasn't ready at all.

He shrugged his coat on, the muscles in his chest and arms flexing beneath his thin shirt. "Okay. Let's do this."

Taking an unsteady breath, I unlocked the door and rushed outside in vamp speed, shocked when Alex appeared beside me the moment I stopped.

How did he do that? Was it a witch thing? A magic thing? I'd never seen a witch move that fast.

But there was no time for questions now. Locking the club while Alex scanned the surrounding area, I waited for him to give the okay before we moved away from the warded building, just in case we had to hightail it back inside.

Whatever it was that had come after me earlier, its presence wasn't nearly as strong as it had been the first time I'd stepped outside. Either it had just left, or it was still here, but far enough away so as not to be an immediate threat.

Alex grabbed my hand. "Let's go."

Without thinking too much about it, I gripped his large palm and followed. I still didn't fully trust this male, even though there was no reason that I shouldn't. Not really. I mean, he'd saved my life, but that had been a deal struck between Killian and Judy, the High Priestess. The witch coven had agreed to help us that one time, and as agreed, they'd done everything they could to save me. Which meant allowing Alex to use his magic on me.

But this time was different.

Now he was acting on his own, coming into our territory without his coven's knowledge, without the consent of Judy or Killian.

I came up with many reasons why he would do what he was doing, and discarded them just as quickly as they appeared. None of it made sense. Why would he take such a risk?

I know what he'd told me the first night he'd come to check on me. And I know what he'd told me tonight. But although I was trusting him with my life, I just had a hard time believing he didn't have some kind of ulterior motive.

I glanced at him from the corner of my eye. He still held my hand with an iron grip. Strong, even for a human. Luckily, the chances were super slim any of the guys would still be out and about this close to sunrise. As a younger vampire—at least compared to the rest of the group—I didn't have the authority to give Alex permission to be alone with me. And I didn't have the power to challenge Killian over his right to be here if we were caught together.

Alex walked with his eyes straight ahead, looking neither right nor left, seemingly unconcerned. But I wasn't fooled. I could feel the magic surrounding him. Felt it slithering over my hair and skin as it probed the air around us, searching for anything out of the ordinary.

I shivered, and Alex glanced over at me, his brows lowered and his eyes concerned. I gave him a tight smile but said nothing.

He was right. What he'd said before. His magic was different from the others. Darker or something. It frightened me, if I was being honest. Not that all magic wasn't scary when it was on the defensive, but the aura emitting from Alex was like nothing I'd ever experienced before.

Yet, still. Something drew me to him. Something I couldn't explain.

My cell phone buzzed in my pocket. Releasing Alex's hand, I pulled it out without slowing my pace. It was Killian. I showed the screen to Alex and answered the call. "Hey, Killian...Yeah, I'm heading that way right now. Yup. I'm hurrying. See you in a few." Disconnecting the call, I put my phone back into my pocket.

Without a word between us, we gripped each other's hand again and picked up the pace.

New Orleans was just starting to wake up, and I came to the conclusion that Alex must've been right when he'd said the people would keep away the threat. Although The Quarter wasn't near as crowded as it was at night, the humans who lived here year round still needed to work their day jobs and were beginning to fill the streets, even at this early hour.

When we got to within a block of the two-story house I shared with the other vampires, I pulled Alex into a doorway. With a hand against his chest, I kept him there. "You shouldn't come any closer. Killian is still awake. He might see you. And even if he doesn't, he'll sense you."

"Watching out the window like an overbearing father?" Although his tone was teasing, his expression was almost...angry.

I didn't understand what it was about this situation that would make him feel like that. He'd been around us vampires long enough to know how it worked. Killian created me. He was the master of the coven. And we stuck around as long as he would have us, because as a master vampire, he had power far exceeding any of ours. We watched out for him and gave him a family, and he protected us and gave us a home. It was a win-win situation. "He very well might be."

I kept my own tone light. But when he didn't seem amused, I sighed. My skin was prickling with the oncoming sunrise. I didn't have time for this. "I have to get inside," I told him.

His eyes shot up to the sky, as though it had only just occurred to him how late—or early, depending on how you looked at it—it was.

"Please, Alex, just stay here." His golden eyes found mine again. I could see the turbulence within them as his desire to see me all the way home dueled with his instinct to keep himself alive. "Don't come any closer. I appreciate everything you've done tonight; I really do. And I don't want anything to happen to you."

After a long pause, he finally nodded. "I'll stay here. But as soon as you get inside, keep everyone away from the windows."

I frowned and shook my head. "Alex, you need to go home before you're discovered here."

I felt a brush of skin against my left hand and looked down to find his fingers playing with mine. I gripped his hand and held on tight, suddenly afraid for him.

"I'm not leaving until I put a ward around your house. It'll only taking me a few minutes and I should do it now while there aren't that many people on the streets."

He cupped my cheek with his free hand, his eyes searching my face. I had the feeling he wanted to say something more, but in the end, he dropped his hand and released my fingers. "Go. Before you're caught in the sun. I'll watch from here until you're safely inside. I'll give you one minute to get everyone's attention, and then I'm coming to ward the house."

I nodded. "Fine." With one last look at my unlikely savior, I turned to walk away, and paused. "Thank you," I told him earnestly. Pressing a quick kiss to his cheek, I hurried down the sidewalk.

My cheeks burned with embarrassment. I'd wanted to convey my honest gratefulness. But the look on his face right before I'd run away told me I may have overstepped my bounds.

Gods, I was such an idiot.

I rushed through the back door just as I felt the heat of the sun on my back. Quickly, I shut it and turned the lock before I stepped away from the window. My reaction was kind of silly. Every window in this house was treated, the sun couldn't hurt me once I was inside. And it would take a bomb to break them. I knew this, but my instincts still forced me to stay out of the direct rays.

"Kenya! Where the fuck have you been?"

Pasting a smile on my face, I turned to face Killian. "Hey, Killian!"

My creator and friend strode toward me. He wasn't a big guy. Not like Alex. But anyone with half a wit about them would know Killian was just as dangerous. His power, fueled by his anger, coiled around him like a serpent, tightly leashed but ready to strike at a moment's notice. He'd always been protective, but ever since my brush with the true death, he really had been like an overbearing father. "Don't give me that smile, acting like you didn't just almost kill yourself in the sunlight."

I heaved a sigh. If the heaviness of his Irish accent was any indication, he was past angry and on to worried sick. "I'm sorry." Walking past him, I led him to the kitchen in the center of the house. He would still be able to see out the front windows if he was looking, but what I was about to tell him should hold his attention long enough to allow Alex to do his thing. "Where's Lizzy?" I liked Killian's new mate, and she was the only one who could calm him down these days when he got himself all in a tizzy.

He didn't respond to my question, though he did look down the hall toward their bedroom, unable to resist. "You told me you were finishing up two hours ago."

"Yeah, I know. I had a visitor."

His head snapped around.

That had gotten his attention.

"Who?" he demanded. "A customer?" Sometimes, the ladies who'd had an especially memorable night at our club with one of the guys—usually Brogan—tried to come back after closing to see if the fun time they'd had could develop into something more.

Spoiler alert: It never did.

I shook my head as I went over to the cabinet to grab a glass. I'd just downed half a bottle of vodka, but alcohol didn't hang around long in a vampire's system, and I needed something to calm my nerves. And the way Killian was staring daggers at me, it would keep his attention on me and not on the warlock I'd just spotted outside the windows behind him.

Alex stared at me for a brief second, then his mouth began moving silently as he warded the house.

"Whiskey?" I offered Killian.

He gave me a nod, and I grabbed him a glass, too.

"Who came to the club then?" Killian asked again.

I set the glass in front of him and talked while I poured us each a shot of his favorite whiskey. "I don't know. I didn't see them."

He held up his hand to stop my pour and I moved on to my own glass. Then he waited until I'd set down the bottle and picked up my glass before he gave me what I called his "expectant face."

I leaned back against the cabinets and looked at him across the island. "When I went to leave, I'd just gotten outside and locked up when I felt someone watching me. But I didn't see anyone. Just the usual humans stumbling back to their hotels."

"Are you sure someone was there?"

He wasn't patronizing me. Killian would never do that. He respected my intelligence, if not my ability to look after myself.

And honestly, I couldn't really blame him there. I had been an awkward human, and I was more times than not a complete failure as a vampire. Besides my eyesight never correcting itself, I didn't appreciate any of the things my new life as a supernatural creature could give me, preferring to stay home and read when I wasn't at work. I didn't even enjoy the excitement of the hunt. I got my meals from the women the guys lured into our private room.

Honestly, I was surprised Killian had kept me after he'd turned me.

To answer his question, I gave him a nod and took another drink. "Mm-hmm. I felt it, Killian. The hatred. The sorcery. But it wasn't one of Judy's coven." Having lived so close to them for so many years, we were all familiar with the feel of that particular group of witches.

His drink sat on the counter, forgotten. "Why the fuck didn't you call me?"

"Because I didn't want anything to happen to you." This was true. Although I believed, ultimately, Killian might be able to overtake Alex if he could get past his warlock's spells, he would not be able to defeat the entire coven of witches who would come to get their revenge if he hurt one of their own. They would force him out into the sun and burn him alive.

If he was lucky.

"It was something really dark, Killian. And it felt horribly familiar." My voice was thick with tears and the fear I finally allowed myself to feel.

In a flash, he was around the counter and holding me in his arms, one hand pressing my head to his shoulder. "You should've called me," he insisted.

I started to tremble as the events of the night hit me all at once. I was scared. A hell of a lot more scared than I'd let on to Alex.

A wave of anger surrounded me, but only for a moment before it was quickly retracted.

Wait. That wasn't Killian.

Opening my eyes, I met the furious glare of Alex through the glass. Widening my eyes, I lifted my hand and waved him away.

"What's going on?" a female voice said.

I quickly gripped Killian again and let myself take comfort in my maker's arms for a few more seconds before I pulled away, stealing a quick glance out the window to make sure Alex had left, and faced Lizzy, Killian's mate. "I'm sorry," I told her. "I had a rough night."

"Someone came after Kenya tonight," Killian spoke over me, his hands still on my arms.

Immediately, she was by my side. Her hands joined her mate's as she looked me over, panic in her pretty brown eyes. "Oh, my God. Kenya! Are you okay? Did anything happen? Why didn't you call me?"

Even the new witch who knew practically nothing about magic was offering to protect me. "I'm fine," I told her. "I went back inside the club and locked myself in until it was safe to come home."

Killian stepped away and gave me up to Lizzy's concern. Her dark hair was in wild disarray, she had no makeup on, and she was wearing a T-shirt that was too big on her—Killian's, if I remembered correctly. She was still stunning.

"What were you thinking?" he asked me. "Locking yourself in the club was probably the worst thing you could've done."

"Apparently not. Because it worked," I told him. "I just waited it out, and eventually it left." I shrugged. "He clearly didn't want to be seen by any residents of the city."

"You know it's a him, then?"

"No, I don't," I told him honestly. "But that's the feeling I got. Maybe it was just all of the frustration and anger."

Lizzy harrumphed, earning her a look from the lone male in the room before he turned back to me.

"And he just left?" Killian asked. "Just like that?"

"Could it be another vampire?" Lizzy said. "I'm just thinking with the sun coming up, that maybe that's why they left." She shrugged as though to say *I got nothing else.* "Is there anyone else who's sensitive to sunlight?"

Killian and I both shook our heads. "Not that I'm aware of," he told her. Chewing on the inside of his cheek, he crossed his arms over his middle and paced away.

Lizzy turned me toward her. "I'm so glad you're okay."

I returned her smile. "Yeah, me too."

"I wish I could stay with you, but I need to get ready to go to the voodoo shop."

She gave me one last, quick hug and made to rush off, but Killian suddenly appeared in front of her. Lizzy crashed into his chest and his hands shot out to steady her. "I don't want you going there today," he told her.

"Killian, I have to. Mike can't make it. I gave him some time off."

"Take it back and tell him to go in."

She rolled her eyes. "I'm not going to do that."

"I can't protect you during the day," he gritted out. "I can't be there with you. And that thing is here, in our city."

Lizzy stopped trying to get around him and let him pull her against his chest, mumbling words of reassurance to her mate.

While they were distracted with each other, I wandered closer to the doorway that led to the front room, searching through the windows for Alex, but he was nowhere to be seen. I didn't dare leave the room though, even as exhausted as I was. I knew Killian wasn't finished with me.

When it sounded like they'd reached a compromise—translated into Lizzy going to the shop as she wanted to and Killian having to deal with it or tie her to the bed—I refilled my whiskey and settled onto one of the kitchen stools.

A few minutes later, Killian joined me and I told him everything that had happened in more detail.

Well, almost everything.

Now, I just had to hope Alex would also keep silent about where he was and who he was with tonight.

4

THE DJINN

I pulled up in front of the pile of lumber and sheet metal that used to be a house of sorts. The house the vampire should have died in.

However, I was so very glad she hadn't.

Her illness had been a test I'd created. Taking a spell I'd found and infusing it with my own very different kind of magic, I had hoped it would be enough to take out a vampire. I had two reasons for doing this. The first was mostly for fun, because the blood suckers insisted on continuing to mate with the witches who should ultimately be in MY coven. Not theirs. However, a vampire's blood bond was impossible to break, so there was no hope of severing it once they'd been fed on by their leach of a mate.

That is, unless one side of that bond no longer existed.

But unlike the vampires, if the witch was left alive, their physical body would just pick up its natural course where it had left off. They would begin to age naturally again, no worse the wear for their little trip to the immortal side. However, I'd learned from experience that this approach did nothing to bond the witches to me. Actually, they took extreme offense when I released them from the mating bond. Something that left me flabbergasted, to say the least.

On the flip side, however, a vampire would die without its mate's blood, but I certainly couldn't run around killing off the witches I wanted to recruit. That made no sense at all.

I'd needed another way. Something I wouldn't be blamed for.

The second, more important reason, to leave the safety of my home and do what I'd done was much more personal. It had to do with my own blood. Family I'd been denied and who I hadn't even known existed until I'd been tipped off that one of the witches here in the wonderful city of New Orleans had magic that was quite a bit...different. Darker, like my own. I'd needed a way to flush them out without scaring them away.

The curse I'd created was effective, but obviously took entirely too long to finish the job. This ended up being a good thing, for it gave the others time to figure out a cure. And that's exactly what had happened. I knew a simple warlock would be unable to undo a djinn's magic. And I'd been correct. The vampire's savior hadn't been a simple witch.

He was only part warlock.

And part djinn.

My new problem was that he was obviously quite taken with the vampire he'd saved, as he'd so happily proven to me tonight. But actually, that had also turned out to be a good thing. His little act of rebellion had revealed something to me. Something I never would have known otherwise.

Running my tongue over the roof of my mouth, I could still taste the voodoo in her blood. In her frantic haste to get back inside of the club, the vampire had cut herself, leaving behind this gift for me to find. Just a drop. But that was all that I'd needed. I wondered if she was even aware of the legacy she carried within her. Of what she was capable of.

If I'd known who she was, I never would have tried to kill her that first time. But it had been so easy to see how adored and protected the female was by the other vampires. Like a little sister. An easy target, if an unwilling sacrifice.

I also knew witches and vampires could not live in such close proximity to each other without some type of truce between them. And if history was any indicator, it would be an agreement of mutual benefit to them both. Which I deduced to mean that when the chips were down for one group, they wouldn't hesitate to enlist the help of the other. And only one of the witches would have the talent to withdraw my curse.

One who was like me.

Imagine my surprise when I discovered there were two.

When my source here had told me the vampire had been cured, I didn't dare to believe. But now that my great niece and nephew had been revealed to me, I could do what I'd come back here to do: convince them to come back to the north with me where they belong. Or they would soon discover they are on the wrong side of the battlefield. For when their coven of witches discovered whose blood ran through their veins, they would no longer be welcome. They would become too much of a threat.

And now, there was the vampire...

Her blood sweet on my tongue, I got out of the car and went inside the house where my source had assured me I would be undisturbed. Although most of the back had been destroyed by weather, the front of it was still intact. And as it was barely habitable anymore, I highly doubted anyone would mind me using it for the brief time I would be here.

Inside, I took off my long, black coat and hung it by the door. Hands linked behind my back, I wandered over to the side window to watch the sun rise over the swamp and think of how I was going to get a vampire away from her master. A feat that was nigh impossible and not without great risk, but one someone like me could overcome.

The harder part was going to convince Alex and Alice that their place was with me.

Alice.

The name brought up memories I would rather forget. Memories of another woman with that name, also a witch, who I'd had wrapped around my finger for a time.

Or, I would have if it hadn't been for that insolent brother of mine.

Victor had wanted her for his own, and, somehow, he had convinced her that I was the bad guy in that whole scenario. And just when I'd managed to talk her into using her magic to bring me into this world, they'd quickly sent me back to my own. Fools that they were, distracted by their fairytale happily ever after, they'd expected me to stay there.

Forty years later, I came back and killed them both. Then, I took over Alice's coven.

In that time, they'd had children, who also had children. By this time, unhappy with my rule, some of the witches had scattered, leaving their mountain outside of Seattle. One of those witches had born the twins I'd now just discovered here, in New Orleans, far from the home of their birth. Direct descendants of my brother, Victor, and his love, Alice.

My blood. My family.

The man, Alex, I'd been told was the one who'd removed my curse from the vampire.

What I hadn't counted on was his continued protection of the female vampire. I'd decided she was too much of a distraction, one that needed to be removed. I didn't want him to have anything else that would tie him to this place. But all things happened for a reason. If last night's occurrences hadn't occurred exactly how they had, I would not have tasted her blood. And I would not now know what I did...

That this vampire could bring back my Alice. I admit, I'd been hasty in my anger when I'd killed her, for I missed her more than I ever thought I would.

So, I will bring her back. With the two of us ruling side by side and my niece and nephew back where they belong, none would be more powerful. Every other coven in the world would have to come into our fold or be extinguished. No other creature, supernatural or otherwise, would be able to touch us.

We would be immortal.

We would be all powerful.

We would rule the fucking world.

All I needed was the vampire with voodoo in her blood. And my nephew would be the one to bring her to me.

5

ALEX

My sister, Alice, was waiting for me when I got home. I wasn't surprised. She was a strong witch. A locked door did little to keep her out when she really wanted to get in somewhere.

I hardly spared her a glance, sitting prettily on the edge of the couch in my small apartment, fingers laced together on her lap. As usual, she wore what our mother would've called "hippie" clothes, all loose and flowing and bright.

I rather liked that look on her though. It suited her.

Taking off my coat, I tossed it onto the back of a kitchen chair. "I'm tired, Alice. What is it that you want?"

"What are you doing?" she asked.

"I would like to go to bed, except my annoying sister has made it a habit to break into my home and keep me awake with her incessant questions."

"It's morning."

"I can see that," I told her, indicating the daylight coming through the single window.

My home was a tiny, one bedroom apartment on Saint Charles Ave in The Garden District. It wasn't much to look at with its fake wood floors and beige walls, but it was clean. And it was mine. And I didn't need much. There was a tiny coat closet by the entry door and another, only slightly bigger closet, in the bedroom. The kitchen was shoved into a small hallway that connected the entry to the living room and consisted of a white sink, a small, white oven, and a miniature refrigerator. There were three white cabinets above the sink, and maybe a foot of counter space made of some sort of ugly, brown laminate taken up by a microwave that took care of most of my meals.

Luckily, I wasn't much of a cook.

My bedroom, if you could call it that, had an air conditioner shoved into the window. And when it came on, it shook the entire building. A queen-sized bed was squeezed into the corner, and that left me just enough room to open the closet doors where I stashed my clothes and my camera equipment.

The old, black, leather couch my sister sat on was the only other furniture, other than the secondhand TV near the window. I hardly ever watched it. It wasn't much, but it was enough for me.

By the way she perched on the edge, careful not to touch any more of the cushion than she had to, Alice gave off the distinct impression that she did not agree. "You could've just called," I told her.

"So you could ignore my phone calls and messages?"

With a sigh, I grabbed a couple of beers from the fridge and sat down beside her, offering her one.

"Alex, it's barely past sunrise. And don't you have to work today?"

"No. I'm between gigs." Winters were slow for me. "And your point?" I asked, offering the beer again.

She stared at me with what I like to call her "mom stare," because it was the same look our mother used to give me before she died and left the two of us alone. Well, not exactly alone. We had Judy, and the coven. And we had each other.

Her expression softened, and her brown eyes filled with concern.

Gods. Here we fucking go.

"Alex, I'm worried about you."

"And why is that, Alice? What the fuck are you worried about this time?"

"Your obsession with the female vampire," she told me bluntly.

That was one thing I liked about my sister. She didn't waste my time. Or anyone else's, for that matter.

"Kenya," I said.

"What?"

"Her name is Kenya." I took a long swig of my beer, trying to fight down the reaction I had just mentioning her name.

"All right. *Kenya*," she repeated. "I'm worried about your obsession with her." She paused. "I know where you were all night."

"If you know that, then you also know why I was there."

"It's not up to you to protect her, Alex. She's just a vampire."

I exploded up off the couch. "Jesus Christ, Alice! Stop fucking saying that." We'd had this same conversation when she first found out I was hanging around the outskirts of The Quarter in my free time.

Luckily, she was used to my moods, and hardly reacted anymore. "It's true. She's not your concern."

Finishing off the bottle I was on, I set it down on the TV stand and popped the cap off the other one. "She wouldn't even exist right now if it wasn't for me."

"That doesn't make her yours."

I stilled. I couldn't look at her. Because that's exactly how I felt. My lovely sister had nailed it on the head with a few softly spoken words. "I never said she was."

Her skirt rustled as she stood and made her way over to me, putting her face in my line of vision until I had no choice but to look at her. "Alex, you're my brother. You're all I have left. Getting involved with the vamp...with Kenya," she corrected, "will cause you nothing but a whole lot of trouble. It may even get you kicked out of the coven, if her master doesn't kill you first."

"Killian is mated to a witch."

"A witch who isn't part of our coven. At least, not officially. And do you honestly think that will make him—or Aunt Judy—more lenient?"

I searched her delicate face, so like my own, and yet at the same time so different. I didn't want to think about Killian or Kenya's blood tie to him. "How did you know?" I asked her, giving up the pretense.

One side of her mouth lifted in a patronizing smile. "How do you know what I'm feeling all the time?"

Tipping the bottle to my mouth, I chugged down half of it before I could meet her eyes again, and changed the subject. "Why do you think that is, Alice?"

She shrugged. "It's a twin thing. It's always been like this with us." She shoved at my shoulder playfully. "It's the same reason I'm not afraid of your temper." Her expression got serious. "I know it's only because you feel things so deeply, Alex. And sometimes it's too much for you, and it has to come out."

But I shook my head. "It's more than that. And don't try to tell me it's not."

"Your temper?"

"No. You know what I mean."

Alice just looked at me with that patient expression of hers, the one that made me want to scream in her face.

Instead, I cocked my head to the side, regarding my sister with narrowed eyes. "Do you really believe this is just normal magic? And don't fucking lie to me. Because you know damn well there's something else with you and me, Alice. Something within us that's not the same as the rest of the family." I paced to the window and back, unable to stand still. "Not one witch was able to help Kenya at the swamp that night, Alice. Not fucking *one*. Even Judy, who, as the High Priestess, is supposed to be not only the eldest but the most powerful, didn't know what to do." I leaned down into her face. "*I* did, Alice. *I* knew what to do."

She backed away. Not because I was in her face, I knew better than that, but to hide her own. "It was a lucky draw—"

"No! It was more than that and you fucking know it. It was,"— I looked around the room, desperately searching for an explanation on the beige walls—"I don't know. Instinct. Something dark inside of me that responded to the evil inside of her. I'd sensed it before that night, but I'd never tried to tap into it."

"Why not?" she challenged. "If it's been there all along, why haven't you tried to harness it before now?"

She didn't believe me. "Because I was fucking scared," I told her gruffly, afraid if I said the words too loud the shit inside of me would hear and make itself known, just to fuck with me. "And stop acting like you didn't feel it, too. We were linked. All of us were linked. There's no way I could have done what I did without drawing on the magic of the entire coven. So don't stand there and act like you don't know what the hell I'm talking about."

"If you're so sure about this, why are you just saying this to me now, brother? It's been weeks."

I shook my head. I didn't know.

"Because you've been too busy obsessing about your vampire," she answered for me, getting back to her original subject. "You have to stop, Alex. You can't just go to the vampire's club by yourself without permission. If you get caught sneaking around to see that vampire, the peace between our covens will be over."

I didn't bother to ask her how she knew where I was. It was obvious now why she was here, other than to lecture me. She'd needed something of mine to do a tracking spell. "How long have you been here tracking me?"

"Long enough to know you had the balls to not only go to The Purple Fang, but to go to their house. Their *home*, Alex. How would that not have come off as a threat if you'd been caught?"

"I wasn't caught."

"But. What. If. You. *Were.*"

Finishing my beer, I went to the fridge and grabbed another. She was right. She was completely fucking right. If I'd been caught, there would've been no getting out of it. I doubted Killian would've listened to Kenya long enough to give her a chance to fight for my life, even if she would have.

As I stood staring into the open fridge with a cold beer in my hand, I felt my sister's touch on my arm. Turning my head, I looked down at her, letting her see the anguish on my face. She was the only one I ever exposed myself to like this. "I had to do something. Whatever had come after her the first time is back. It's here, in New Orleans. And it's not here to sightsee. It's here for her."

"Perhaps you should just let it have her."

She didn't mean it in a hateful way. I could feel her emotions nearly as well as my own, and they were as heavy as mine. She was only trying to keep me safe. To keep our coven safe.

"You've always been so hard to control," she told me. "But you have to remember, Alex, it's not just you. It's all of us."

"You have it, too," I told her. "Stop skirting around the subject. I feel it within you, Alice. It's not as strong, but it's there."

"Alex. Stop."

"I felt it that night at the swamp. The darkness in you flowing through the coven's combined magic. It fed into mine. It helped me grab onto the ugliness inside of Kenya and rip it out. There's no way I could've held onto it without your help. She would've died. Kenya would've died." My voice broke and I turned away. Embarrassed.

"But she didn't." Alice squeezed my arm. "However you did it, however *we* did it, doesn't matter. We saved her, and we prevented the war that surely would've started if Killian had lost one of his most precious possessions. Because that's exactly what she is, and what would've happened. In his grief, he would've come after us, and the rest of his vampires would've reacted the same. It was why Aunt Judy was so determined to stay out of it to begin with, until Lizzy convinced her otherwise."

Closing the door to the fridge, I turned around and leaned up against it. "Why won't you just admit it?"

She held her hands out, genuinely confused. "Admit what, Alex? That we have some imaginary demon magic inside of us?"

With a frustrated sigh, I looked away.

"Look," she told me. "All I'm asking is that you think of the rest of us before you go running off to try to be the night in shining armor to a female who does not need your help."

"She needed it tonight."

"She won't anymore. I'm sure she's telling her master all about it even as we speak."

"Gods, Alice! Stop calling him that."

"Why? That's what he is. And you'd do well to remember it."

I was growing tired of this conversation. If she wasn't who she was, I would've kicked her out long before now. "I need some sleep."

Though I wouldn't look at her, I felt her eyes searching my face for a long moment before she finally said, "Okay. I'll go. But...just think about what I said. And stay the hell out of The Quarter, Alex."

I nodded, letting her know I heard what she was saying, but neither confirming nor denying I would do either one.

Following her to the door, I grabbed her arm before she could leave. "And when you're ready to talk about the fact that there's something else going on with us, feel free to come break into my apartment again so we can try to figure out what the hell it is and what it means for us."

"I didn't break in," she deflected.

"Do you have a key?" I asked.

She stared up at me with big, guileless, brown eyes. "If you didn't want me in here, you'd ward the apartment to keep me out."

A laugh broke out from my chest. Grabbing the back of her head, I pulled her toward me and dropped a kiss on her honey-blonde hair. "Now get out."

Opening the door, she stepped out into the hallway. "Don't forget we have a thing tomorrow night at Aunt Judy's."

"I'll be there."

Closing the door behind her, I threw the lock. Out of respect for my sister, I'd think about what she'd said. It wouldn't keep me away from Kenya, but I'd think about it.

I was already feeling uneasy being so far away from her.

6

LUUKAS KREEK, MASTER VAMPIRE SEATTLE, WA

I stared through my apartment window at the lights of Seattle, concentrating on my breathing. Taking a deep inhale and then slowly releasing the breath, I focused on the beauty outside and attempted to slow my heart rate.

I'd loved my city since the moment I'd first set foot in it. Even now, in the state my head was in, it would be remiss of me not to acknowledge she was even more beautiful after the invention of electricity.

However, these days it was a struggle to find any appreciation for the view that had always brought me so much peace.

With the side of my closed fist, I swiped at the bedroom window, foggy from the rain, though logically I knew it would do no good.

My emotions churned out of control.

Closing my eyes, I pressed both palms against the cool glass. Was I dreaming? It was difficult for me to decipher the prison of my mind from reality at times...

Still. After all these months.

Flashes of bloodstains and the stench of burning flesh assaulted my senses. My flesh. My head fell forward, the sting of my fangs punching down as my fingertips slid along the smooth glass, trying to find something to anchor me in my new reality.

Slowly, gradually, the horrors faded. I lifted my head, and the city came back into focus. I took another deep breath. Then another. And another. It did little to calm my racing heart.

Rubbing my damp palms on my bare thighs, I glanced over at my witch, asleep on the bed. The sun would be up soon, and she was passed out hard, oblivious to my loss of control. Her long hair was a dark cloud across her pillow, one arm flung out as though searching for me even in her sleep. I listened to her soft breathing as my eyes travelled over the smooth skin of her back and shoulders. I matched my breath with hers, and finally, my racing heart settled into a more normal rhythm.

MINE.

I felt that truth with every fiber of my being, and it both energized and terrorized me. Keira was my witch. And it shamed me that, at times, when I was in a particularly dark place, my broken spirit demanded retribution for the years of complete and utter hell she had put me through. Luckily, I was a mated vampire, and those instincts would never allow me to harm her.

Because she was also my angel. The one who had saved me from the hell of my own mind. Keira owned my heart, my body, and my soul, but perhaps not all of me. Not yet.

Today, I was grateful she slept. She worried about me, with good fucking reason, and she didn't get as much rest as she should.

Turning on my heel, I left her naked in my bed and went to the closet to pull on a pair of flannel pants and a T-shirt. There was no need to wake her for this. I was barely holding it together as it was. If she were involved…

Barefoot, I padded silently out of the bedroom, shutting the door quietly behind me.

The warlock was waiting for me, sprawled casually in my favorite armchair. The fact that he was already inside the locked apartment caught me off guard, though it shouldn't have.

Jesse's appearance was much changed without the hooded robe he liked to hide within. But even in black dress slacks and a dark short-sleeved pullover shirt, his aura oozed power. He, like myself just moments before, stared out at the lights of the city, his golden eyes burnished with memories of other places and times.

I walked past without acknowledging the warlock's presence, trying—and failing—to ignore the chills that raced across my skin when the male rose and followed me into my glass-walled office. I hadn't been this close in proximity to the other male since the night we'd sent the demons back to hell. And there'd been too much activity that night for anyone except Keira to notice my weakness.

When Jesse joined me inside, I closed the door, flinching when the latch clicked into place. The mechanism resounded in my eardrums loud as a bomb, and I had to remind himself of where I was. I left the lights off, not wanting to startle Keira if she happened to wake and came looking for me. Taking my seat behind the desk, I struggled to keep my hands from tightening into fists as I waited for the other male to speak. Not that it would matter if he saw. The warlock could sense my fear. And it was nothing I could help.

But it was a matter of pride.

Jesse pressed the tips of his fingers together under his chin and regarded me calmly. "So, we are doing this in secret?"

"For now." My voice sounded sure and even, and for that much I was grateful.

A smile teased the corners of the warlock's mouth. "There's no need for such subterfuge, vampire."

Vampire. I repressed a shudder as shards of ice slid up and down my spine. Flashes of terror, too sharp and too horrifying to be called memories, crashed through my mind. My teeth began to hurt and I felt a sting as my fangs left punctures inside my lower lip. With great effort, I released the tension in my jaw. This was the first time I'd been truly alone with the warlock since Leeha's dungeon.

I wondered if I would always react this way when we were in the same room.

Jesse cocked his head to the side, narrowing his eyes, peering straight into my deepest secrets. Or so it felt. Then he sighed with impatience. "There's no need to fear me, Luukas."

There was no sense in trying to deny it. "Is there not?"

"No." Jesse's tone was final. "Shea would never forgive me if I ever did anything to harm you or the others. And for her, I would do absolutely anything. Even give up my only chance at besting my father." He paused, and my mind went back to that night we sent Jesse's demons back to hell. "However, know that if any of you hurt her—physically or emotionally—I won't hesitate to protect her."

The warlock's condescending tone struck a chord and I found myself leaning forward in my chair, upper lip lifted to bare my fangs. Anger, rather than fear, drove my movements this time. "Shea was part of this family long before she met you, warlock. And she will be a part of this family long after you're gone from her life. Don't think to sit here and threaten me or my vampires in my own home."

Jesse leaned back in his chair and smiled. "And there's the male I met all those years ago. Before Leeha broke you."

"Leeha did not break me." I stared him right in the eye. "But you nearly did." The words stuck in my throat, and I wondered why I would admit anything to this male, especially a weakness. But perhaps admitting it was the first step to recovery?

One side of the warlock's mouth lifted in something resembling a smile as he rubbed his forehead with the tips of his fingers, but there was no humor in his eyes. "This isn't getting us anywhere," he muttered. Taking another deep breath, he met my steady gaze. "The past is what it is, vampire. I did what I believed I needed to do at the time. And I won't apologize for it. I'm sure there are similar things you've done in your past?" He paused, waiting expectantly. When no answer was forthcoming, he rolled his eyes and continued, "Can we not try to move forward? I am on Shea's side, which means I am on your side. And, as you well know, I can be quite the ally to have."

"Yes. As long as you remain my ally."

"You have my word."

"As long as Shea is alive."

That twist of his lips was back. "That is correct."

I sheathed my fangs. The male was right. Having him on our side would only be a boon to us. However, I would never trust him as I did the others. Still...

"I guess that will have to be good enough."

Jesse sat forward in his chair. "Now that we've talked about our feelings, can we get down to the business of killing my father?"

I gave him a nod.

Jesse stood and wandered over to the windows. The sun would be coming up any minute now, but its lethal rays posed no danger to me. The windows were treated to protect us from it, and nothing short of Godzilla could break them.

He turned away from the cityscape and faced me. "Well, vampire? What's the plan?" As I opened my mouth to speak, Jesse held up one hand, his head tilted slightly as though he were listening to something.

He'd done this a lot when we'd spent time together in the dungeon. He was listening to the voices that whispered in his ear.

"Wait, wait. Yes, I forgot. There's something else you need to know before we start."

I crossed my arms over my chest and leaned back in my chair. "And what is that?"

By the look he gave me, Jesse wasn't fooled by my calm façade, and he also didn't seem surprised. I knew he could hear my rushing pulse, my heart beating hard and fast within my chest. The rage that had driven me when I'd escaped the dungeon was gone, and the insanity that came with it was swiftly following in its footsteps, though it still had a tenuous hold on me.

And that, more than anything else, was what still gave Jesse the power.

But, for now, he needed me. Because without me, the others would not follow.

Jesse waved his hand in the air and refocused on me, his golden eyes the same eyes that haunted my nightmares. "I need to tell you about Ryan."

I frowned. "Ryan? Christian's mate?"

Jesse gave me a nod.

"What about her?" I narrowed my gaze on Jesse, allowing him to see the mistrust in my eyes though my expression remained controlled.

"She is my sister." With that piece of information out in the world, he turned back to the window as I processed what he'd just said.

Ryan? That wasn't possible.

After a long moment, I said, "I'm sorry. Would you repeat what you just said?"

"She is my sister," Jesse told me again, as the first rays of the morning sun began to lighten the sky. It was truly beautiful after the night's rain, the way it reflected off the buildings. "My twin, actually. Fraternal."

"That means she is—"

"Half djinn and half witch. As am I."

I had no words. However, if I really thought about it, it did make some twisted sort of sense. Ryan heard voices, too, though she had little control over them. Not like the warlock, who seemed to treat them like a group of annoying younger siblings buzzing around him.

"She isn't aware of our relationship," Jesse said. "We were separated shortly after we were born. She doesn't know who I am."

"How do I know you're telling the truth?"

The question was not what he was expecting. "Why would I lie about something like this?"

I leaned one elbow on the arm of my chair, studying Jesse as I rubbed my temple with my fingertips.

"By the way," Jesse said. "My last name is Moss."

I became unnaturally still, the way only a vampire—and perhaps a djinn—could. "What—" Before I could finish the sentence, the most delicious scent assaulted me. My nostrils flared as I breathed it in and my head snapped toward the door.

Keira stood in the open doorway, wrapped in a thin white robe. "What did you say?" she asked. She took a step inside and her voice rose. "What did you just say?"

I stood up so fast my chair flew back into the wall behind me, and from the corner of my eye I saw Jesse watching us with an amused expression as her horrified eyes flew to my face, silently begging me to tell her it wasn't true.

I tilted my chin in the direction of our bedroom. "Keira, go back to bed."

As soon as the words were out of my mouth, I realized my mistake.

She straightened her spine, her stature something I knew well from the time we'd spent together. Dismissing me with a look, I growled low in my throat as she turned her attention back to

Jesse. She ignored me completely. "Did I hear you say your last name is Moss?"

Jesse sat back down in my chair with a sigh. "That's what I said, yes."

A look of horrified understanding dawned across her face. "That makes you my cousin."

"–cousin," he finished at the same time.

Disgust twisted her lovely features. She shook her head in denial, thick, dark hair falling about her shoulders. "That's not possible."

"Ryan is my sister," he repeated for her. "Separated at birth."

She continued to shake her head. "You're full of shit. You're lying."

Jesse rolled his eyes. "As I told your vampire, why would I lie about something like this?"

"I don't know. Why do you do anything you do?"

"I have reasons."

"Fucked up reasons."

I could tell the warlock was swiftly tiring of this conversation. "Enough," he told her. Engaging the spirits hovering around him as I'd seen him do many times before, he had them push her back out of the room and shut the glass door. She ended up on the floor, her robe riding up her thighs.

With a roar of rage, I sprang from my chair, and I heard a satisfying thump as Jesse's head slammed against the wall behind him, my hand around his throat. The glass cracked behind him as I bared my fangs, my eyes burning with rage.

"Do not touch the witch," I hissed at him.

Jesse allowed me my anger, which was surprising, until I heard his next words.

"Because only you are allowed to torture her?"

I began to tremble with rage as he twisted the dagger in my back just a little bit more. The urge to strike was overwhelming.

"Jesse! What are you doing?"

The warlock closed his eyes, and I felt him shiver at Shea's voice. But it wasn't from fear. The scent of his desire for her was strong in my nose.

Moving only his eyes, he looked toward the door and smiled. I followed his gaze, and found her in the open door with her arm around Keira, now back on her feet. Both females were staring at us with similar horrified expressions, but for completely different reasons.

With a wave of his hand, Jesse removed my fingers from his throat and sent me staggering backward.

"Control him, witch," he directed to Keira as I struggled against the power holding me back.

She ran to me without pause, wrapping her arms around my waist and whispering in my ear as she used the physical touch of her body to calm me.

The apartment door crashed open, broken from the hinges by the sounds of it, and Nikulas appeared behind Shea, Aiden on his heels. "What the fuck is going on?"

"Shall we go ahead and call the others?" Jesse asked me.

My attention, focused on the female in my arms, flew back to Jesse. My only response to the question was to hiss at the warlock in warning, but I didn't act on it. Instead, I stayed with my mate, keeping my large body wrapped protectively around her much smaller form.

"Is that a yes?" Jesse looked to Shea for clarification.

She walked over to him, wearing only a long-sleeved cotton shirt and little else if her bare legs and feet were any indication. "Jesse, what's going on? What are you doing?"

He rubbed her cheek with the back of his knuckles. "I only came to speak with Luukas. But things are a little touchy between us, as you can well imagine."

"Talk to him about what?"

"My sister."

Shea's green eyes bore into him. "You don't think you should've told *her* about it first?"

"I didn't want the vampire to think I was plotting behind his back."

"Are you not?" She gave him a steady stare.

Jesse stared into the depths of her eyes for long moments. "No. Not deliberately."

"What are you both blethering on about?" Aiden asked.

Shea took Jesse's hand.

"Yes?" he asked her.

She nodded. "Yes. They all need to know." Still holding his hand, she turned to me. "We should call Dante and Christian. And the rest of the girls. Especially Ryan. She needs to know where she came from. Jesse can help her harness her power."

"Because he does such a wonderful job of it himself?" Nikulas said.

"Nik, please," Shea told him.

Nikulas looked to me, and I gave him a nod. "Okay, then," Nik announced to the room in general. "Aid, will you go get Grace and Emma? I'll round up everyone else."

"Thank you," Jesse told him.

Giving him an uneasy look, Nikulas left the apartment, calling back, "I'll fix this door later, Luuk!"

Aiden followed him out much the way he'd come in.

"And here we go." Shea gave the warlock an uneasy smile.

"It will be all right, Shea. But my father must be stopped. And to do that, I'm going to need Ryan's help."

"I know." Her eyes searched his face. "I just wish we could have a little more time."

Leaning down, he touched his forehead to hers.

I watched their exchange in silence, my witch in my arms, still disbelieving that one of my own could care about something as evil as the warlock. But I'd promised her I'd give him a chance.

We settled in to wait for the others.

7

ALEX

I felt him before I saw him.

Walking to our coven's gathering at my aunt's house at twilight the following night, the air suddenly grew heavy and thick around me. Not an unusual phenomenon living so close to the water, but this wasn't caused by a change in the atmosphere. It wasn't a warning of an oncoming thunderstorm.

No. This was something different.

Something ominous.

The hair all over my body rose as though I were standing in the midst of an electrical storm, but I kept walking, not showing any reaction. I didn't change my pace. I didn't look around. There was no need. I knew what this was. I'd felt it before, the night it came after Kenya.

Only this time, it was coming for me.

The large, waxy leaves of a magnolia tree rustled above me. I glanced at the house it adorned out of the corner of my eye. The two-story Victorian was still, its bay windows dark. I sensed no movement within.

Taking a deep breath to steady myself, I kept my steps at my natural pace. Just like any animal that was being hunted, I knew that showing any hint of fear would only incite the sorcery that was, even now, winding around me. Taking my measure. Trying to get a sense of my power.

Well...let it.

Maybe it would find out I wasn't anyone it wanted to fuck with.

This dark magic followed me for two blocks, and in that time I only saw three other people walking down the street. One a college age kid who carried himself like someone who'd grown up here, and the other two a pair of middle-aged women who were obviously tourists, taking pictures of every other house while gesturing excitedly and sipping on coffees from Cafe Du Monde.

I kept walking, drawing the sorcery away from them before I slipped down a narrow drive between houses, stopped, and waited. I didn't have to wait long.

The man that appeared at the other end was tall and lean with short, brown hair. He wasn't classically good-looking, but there was something about him. Something sensual. Hungry.

Powerful. It was a heady combination. And I wasn't normally into guys.

But something about it wasn't right. It felt wrong. Almost incestuous.

He came sauntering out from behind the houses and stared at me, waiting for me to say something. To question him. To throw a spell at him, maybe. But I wasn't about to give this fucker the satisfaction. No. This bastard was going to come to me. I wanted answers, and I was going to get them tonight. Or I would die trying.

After a few minutes, he shoved his hands into the front pockets of his dark slacks and strolled toward me, his head tilted to the side and a smile playing around his eyes. He wore no coat, only a long-sleeved pullover sweater that looked like it did little to protect him against the night air.

Feet braced apart and arms hanging loose at my sides, I held my ground and watched him come, my body relaxed, my magic dancing along the surface, touching his with tentative fingers.

Through sheer force of will, I kept my heartbeat steady, kept any fear I felt hidden deep down. So deep there was no way he'd ever find it.

"Hello, Alex."

How do you know my name? "Who the fuck are you?"

His brows lowered and the corners of his mouth turned down in an over-exaggerated frown. "Is that any way to greet your uncle?"

At that moment, the wisps of magic that had been feeling me out since he'd first revealed himself to me reached deeper, stretching down my nose and throat, seeping into my pores until it touched the very heart of me. The darkness that bled from the very marrow of my bones.

The demon smiled and my blood froze in my veins. Mostly because I felt no fear, no disgust as his magic mingled with mine. It wasn't foreign to me. It didn't feel like a parasite leeching onto me.

It felt like it belonged there.

"Do you see?" he asked. "You do recognize me even if you don't want to admit it."

This time, I could not control the wave of terror that filled me as I comprehended what he was suggesting. With some effort, I evicted him from my body. At least, that's what it felt like, that *he*, and not just his sorcery, had somehow twisted up inside of me until I was a part of him and he was a part of me. And when I pushed him away, a sense of loss hit me hard, bowing my shoulders for a moment before I was able to straighten to my full height again.

What the fuck was happening?

"What do you want?" I asked him when I could form a cohesive sentence.

"Aren't you the least bit curious?" he wanted to know.

I refused to play his game. "About what, exactly?" I needed time. Time to figure out exactly what this meant. I had entered this driveway ready to fight, to rid Kenya of this threat against her. But unlike the last time, I felt no interest for the vampire coming from him.

Only for me.

Again, he smiled. My changing the rules of his game seemed only to amuse him.

I pushed Kenya from my thoughts, not wanting to draw his attention back to her. It wouldn't surprise me at all if he was able to pull her right from my head and make her appear before my eyes. I didn't know what he was, but he was no ordinary warlock.

I got the distinct impression he wasn't even human.

Lifting one eyebrow, I waited for his answer. But instead of answering my question, he gave me a proposition.

"Let's stop with the games. For now," he added. "Because I do enjoy them immensely. However, we're short on time, and I have an offer for you that I think you'll find hard to refuse."

I played it off, feeling him out. "I seriously doubt that anything you have to say will be of any interest to me."

Strolling up to me until I could see the black specks in his brown eyes, he studied me for an uncomfortable minute before he finally spoke again. "My name is Marcus. And as I told you a few moments ago, I am your uncle. Your great uncle to be exact." Then he frowned. "Or is it great-*great* uncle?" After a moment, he waved a hand through the air. "Eh, it doesn't really matter. The fact of the matter is I'm your family."

How was that even possible? This guy hardly looked any older than me. Only vampires lived that long. And he was no vampire. But I somehow knew that what he was telling me was the truth. Still, I denied it, despite the fact that the lie tasted like metal on my tongue. "You're no blood of mine."

"Oh, but I am, Alex. You see, you and your sister are direct descendants of my brother, Victor."

I didn't know much about my family past my mother, aunt, and cousins who lived here in New Orleans. My father was a mystery to me. Mom would never talk about him.

"Victor's wife, and your great-grandmother, was also named Alice. I imagine that's where your sister gets her name. And she was one of the greatest witches I've ever known." He paused, his eyes clouding over. "They had a daughter, Kim, who then gave birth to your mother."

Alice.

Like my sister.

His expression cleared. "Yes, I'm looking forward to meeting her, too."

I backed up a step, like that would be enough to keep him out of my head. "So, you ARE some kind of vampire." Vamps were the only supernatural creatures I knew of that could read the thoughts right out of your head, sometimes before you even realized you were thinking them.

But he shook his head. "No. I'm not a vampire. No fangs. See?" He bared his teeth at me, and I took another step back.

"What are you then?" I asked him, putting off the whole family talk thing. I suddenly didn't want to know. I seriously didn't. Because as much as I wanted to believe he was lying to me, I knew in my bones that every word coming out of his mouth was the truth. "I know you're not a warlock. And, actually, I have my doubts that you're even human."

"And you would be right."

"So? What are you?"

He paused only for a brief second before he told me. "I'm a djinn."

A djinn.

A fucking djinn.

I'd learned about them, of course. My mother made sure Alice and I were educated not only about math and science and history, but about vampires, shifters, faeries, and yes, djinn. Out of all the creatures we learned about, the djinn scared me the most.

They moved as fast as vampires and could read minds like one, apparently. They were also as strong as vampires, only they practiced magic like witches. No, not magic. Sorcery. Dark sorcery. They played between worlds and could kill a human with a snap of their fingers.

And he was implying that I was one of them. "What do you want from me?" I asked him.

He looked me in the eye. "We're family, Alex. I came to get you and bring you home with me."

Like that was supposed to mean something to me. "I'm not your family."

"You're my blood. You and your sister."

"That doesn't mean shit. I've never met you before tonight. You're a stranger to me." The memory of my magic caressing his made a liar of me, but I pushed those thoughts away. "Besides, I already have a family."

He barked out a laugh. There was no humor in it. "What? Your little coven?"

"Yes," I told him.

"Your High Priestess is an old woman. And she has you all living down here in the swamps and hanging out with vampires because she can't protect you on her own."

"Maybe she just likes the gators."

His mouth turned up at the corners, like he was fighting a smile. Then he shrugged as if to say, *perhaps*.

We stared at each other, neither making a move toward the other.

I didn't know what to think about what he was telling me. I wanted to call him out. Tell him he was lying. And I could.

But then I would be the one lying. I'd felt the connection between us.

This...man...male...*thing*...he was related to me by blood. Of that, I had no doubt. Looking at him now, I could see a bit of my deceased mother in him.

"When did she die?" he asked. "Your mother?"

None of your fucking business was the first thing that came to my mind as an answer to that question. But seeing the expression on his face, I relented. "Last year," I told him. "It happened in her sleep. They think it was an aneurysm." I snapped my mouth shut. What the fuck was I doing?

His eyes fell to the cracked pavement between us and I felt a swell of sorrow hit me like a blast of hot air. Quickly, I raised my shields, cutting his emotions off from me. I was still grieving her. I couldn't handle his emotions, too.

When he raised his head again, there were tears in his eyes. "I'm sorry. I knew her before all of this." He looked at the houses surrounding us. "I wish I could've seen her before..." His words faded away.

"If you've known where we are all this time, why didn't you ever come see us?"

"I didn't know. Not until just recently." He breathed in a long-suffering sigh. "Also, your mother and I had a difference of opinion. Before she had you and your sister," he explained. The smile was back. "She thought humans without powers were our friends. I disagreed."

"What do you think they are?"

Crossing his arms over his chest, his forehead wrinkled up in thought. "Well, if they have certain skills, they can be useful."

"And if they don't?"

He shrugged. "Then they just tend to get in the way."

Uncle or not, I wanted nothing to do with this. With him. I no longer wanted to know about the darkness inside of me. I just wanted it to go away. If would make me like him, I wanted nothing to do with it.

The magic inside of me stirred, reaching for the djinn and denying what I'd just told myself. It took everything I had to pull it back before I gave in.

His head cocked to the side and he studied me. "I'd really like to get to know you and your sister. And I'd love it if you would come stay with me up north."

Somehow, I had the feeling his request wasn't so much a request, but an order. "Why?"

That seemed to catch him off guard. "Why?" he repeated.

"Yeah. Why? Why now? Because I know damn well you didn't just catch a warm, fuzzy feeling of family and suddenly decide to come looking for us. If you really wanted to find us, I think someone such as yourself would've found a way." Something occurred to me, something that might even make all of this make sense. "Unless, you *didn't* know about us. About me and Alice."

His eyes flashed up to mine. It was only for a second. But that second was all I needed to see the truth of it.

"You had no idea about me or my sister until you got here and found us." Or, found me. And I'd played right into his hands by being the one to cure Kenya. By protecting her afterward.

And now I'd given him a much more interesting goal.

Goddammit.

8

KENYA

It was the closing time, and I was just finishing up wiping down the bar at The Purple Fang when my phone buzzed in my pocket. Glancing around, I saw no sign of Jamal. I assumed he went into the back for something, and took a relieved breath.

My phone buzzed again and I pulled it out of the back pocket of my slacks. As I wasn't one of the dancers here, I tried to dress for the part of a bartender at an upscale club. Our place wasn't all that fancy, but it wasn't a dive, either. So, Law of Attraction and all that.

Looking down at the unknown number on the screen, I knew right away who was calling. I silenced the call and put my phone back in my pocket. I couldn't talk to Alex right now. Not while Jamal was here. Even though he was in the back of the club, he would hear everything. Then he would have questions, and I didn't have any answers.

My phone went off again. This time after I silenced the call, I sent him a quick text.

Can't talk right now.

I hadn't seen or spoken to Alex since the night he'd escorted me home and put a ward around the house. Was he still watching out for me? Was it back? There was no other reason he should be taking the risk of calling me. However, I didn't sense anything out of the ordinary.

Jamal came out from the back as I was checking what we had stocked behind the bar.

"Who keeps trying to call you?"

So, he did see me. I shrugged without turning around. "I think it's a wrong number." I felt his eyes on me, boring a hole into my back. He probably sensed my lie. Jamal knew me better than just about anyone. Even Killian.

"Are you sure about that?"

I put a new bottle of Villa One Tequila on the shelf to replace the near empty one and turned around with a smile, wiping my hands on a towel. "Nope. Because I didn't answer the phone."

He narrowed his eyes at me and crossed his arms over his muscular chest, quite obvious through the netted shirt he'd worn tonight as part of his stage attire. Jamal was a favorite with the ladies when he hit the stage. And who could blame them? With his smooth, brown skin and piercing hazel eyes, he was one hell of a good-looking black man. Add in the air of danger he carried about him and the women came a-runnin' from all over New Orleans to see him take it all off. The fact that he could actually dance didn't hurt either.

And on the rare occasions when he smiled...hearts and ovaries had no chance at all. Even my own insides got all fluttery on occasion when he smiled at me.

But right now, he wasn't anywhere close to cracking a grin. "What's going on, Kenya?"

I stopped with the subterfuge. It wasn't any use. If Jamal was determined to get to the bottom of my secrets, he would. So, I needed to give him something. A part of the truth. Just enough to satisfy him. "Remember when I was cursed with some kind of vampire-killing illness and almost died a few weeks ago?"

Anguish twisted his handsome features. "How could I forget?"

I nodded. Stupid question. "Well, whatever it was that did that to me. It came back."

Jamal appeared behind the bar with me, covering a good twenty feet between one second and the next, his hands on my shoulders. "Here? It came here? To the club? Why didn't anyone tell me?"

I nodded again. "When I was closing up a few nights ago. I felt it as soon as I stepped outside to lock up and head home."

"Why the fuck didn't you call me?"

"I didn't know where you were," I answered honestly. "You seemed to hit it off with that blonde who was here with the birthday party and I thought maybe you'd gone off with her. I didn't want to ruin your fun." *Because you have so little of it*, I added silently.

But even as I gave him that excuse, I knew he would call me out on it. Jamal never hooked up with anyone outside of the club. Like, ever.

"That's bullshit, Kenya, and you damn well know it," he said. Releasing my shoulders, he searched my face. "Were you hurt? What happened?"

"I wasn't hurt," I told him as I shook my head. Then I had to push my glasses back up onto my nose, wishing not for the first time that I could wear contacts. But my eyes just wouldn't play nice with anything in them. They were too sensitive now. Just like my skin and my hearing and my sense of smell since becoming a vampire. "I came back inside the club, and after a while, it just...left." I shrugged one shoulder.

"It just left." From his tone, I could tell he was less than convinced.

I nodded.

"It didn't come after you? Didn't try to break in? Nothing?"

"No, although I did sense it right outside at one point."

His brow furrowed. "Why would it just hang around outside like that? It had to know you were in here."

"I don't know." *I did know.* "But it didn't." *Because there's a magical ward around the building to keep it out.*

I'd never been more grateful that Jamal couldn't read minds. Well, not that he couldn't. He could. He just *wouldn't* do it. He didn't like it when any of us were in his head, either. He believed it was an invasion of privacy, and he was right. Being in each other's heads was something we'd all had to learn to control. And the longer you were a vampire, the stronger that power grew. Luckily, our self-control and ability to shield also grew more advanced.

Except against Killian. Maybe because he was the one who'd created us? Or maybe because of how powerful he was. After all, he hadn't become the Master vampire of the region from a vote. If he really set his mind to it, so to speak, there was no keeping him out.

"How did you get home?"

"I just waited it out, and then I walked home." There. All of that was the truth. I'd only neglected to tell him there was someone else here with me. He just wasn't a vampire.

"By yourself?"

"It was gone, Jamal," I told him, avoiding the question.

"Or it was just cloaking itself from you."

Oh gods, that hadn't even crossed my mind. I began to shudder uncontrollably, my emotions, as always, quick to change. "I didn't even think about that." I really hated vampire emotions sometimes.

But, surely, Alex would've still been able to feel it. Right? He was a warlock. Wouldn't he have been able to feel it? He said he could feel it...

Between one breath and the next, I was wrapped up in Jamal's arms. He smelled like cheap, flowery perfume from the lap dances he'd performed tonight, and it was enough to make me wrinkle my nose and ground me into the here and now. Closing my eyes, I returned the hug and allowed myself to feel safe in his arms with his strength wrapped around me. A big brother who would always be there to chase away the bullies. Something I'd never had in my human life.

Instead, I'd had the joy of being bounced around foster homes until I'd gotten too old. Then I was thrown out into the streets to survive on my own. Or not. Nobody had really cared about a nerdy girl who loved to read but didn't have the money for college. A girl who'd barely made the rent on her dingy, one room apartment. A girl who, for the next twelve years of her life, could only get jobs waiting tables or parking cars. Until one night when I'd gotten caught by some nervous muggers walking back to the restaurant where I'd worked after I'd parked a customer's BMW. The gun going off had been an accident. Or, at least, that's what the one guy had screamed to the other after he'd shot me.

And that's when Killian had found me and given me a family.

I heard the distant click of the lock on the front door. Before I even had time to open my eyes and see who it was, Jamal was ripped from my arms so fast his netted shirt was left hanging in my fingers where it had been torn from his body. He slammed into the wall at the back of the club and slid down to the stage, his bare back squeaking on the mirror that covered it.

With a hiss, I tossed Jamal's shirt to the floor and leapt over the bar to face whoever—or whatever—had just come into the club. Landing in a crouch, I immediately rose to my full height again and sheathed my fangs, pushing my glasses up on my nose to make sure I was seeing what I thought I was seeing. "Alex?"

Out of the corner of my eye, I caught a blur of movement and jumped in front of the warlock before Jamal ripped his throat out. "Stop!" I held up my hands, pushing him away from us.

There was a growl behind me, answered by Jamal's hiss.

"Do not touch her," Alex said softly.

A shiver ran up my spine at the possessive timbre of his voice.

Jamal caught it, too, his head tilting to the side as his eyes went from Alex to me and back again. "I'll do whatever the fuck I want with her, witch."

Alex stalked around me, and I caught a glance of his expression from the corner of my eye. It was enough to give me pause. Just for a second, but it was enough to give him time to send Jamal across the room again with nothing but a wave of his hand.

"Alex! Stop!"

He spun toward me so fast I took a step back. "Why was he holding you?" he roared.

Confused, I tried to see around him to check on Jamal, who was back on his feet and heading our way, a murderous expression on his face. If he managed to get ahold of Alex, there was no doubt in my mind he would rip him in half before I could stop him.

Taking a step to the side to put myself between them, I held up my hand. "Jamal, stop. Please. Let me explain."

"He's not the one you should be worrying about right now," Alex told me. "Why was he holding you?"

"Because I was scared," I snapped at him. "Not that it's any of your damned business!"

He stilled, and I felt his magic retract just a bit. "Why?"

This really wasn't the time to get into all of that. "What are you doing here?" I asked him, keeping one eye on Jamal who was pacing silently behind Alex's back, looking for an opening. "Jamal!"

His dark eyes flicked to mine, but he didn't stop moving.

I threw both arms out to the side between the two males. "Jamal, stop. Please. Just...just give me a damn minute."

"Make him leave," Alex ordered. "Or I will."

"You won't lay a hand on him." I stuck my finger in his face in full-on schoolteacher mode.

He wasn't in the least bit intimidated. "I won't have to. He'll never get close enough."

I dropped my arm. Alex was right. Witches were the only ones who had the upper hand on vampires. Taking a risk, I stopped watching Jamal and moved closer to Alex. Something like a purr, or maybe another growl, rumbled in his chest, and I laid my hand over the spot, feeling an answering response shoot through me. "Please, let me explain to him what's going on, and then we can talk."

After a long, tense moment, he gave me a terse nod.

"Thank you." Leaving Alex where he was, I went to Jamal. "Let's go into the back." I knew there was no way he would listen to me with Alex standing right there, just begging for a fight. "Come on, Jamal." I walked away, heading toward the back office and hoping he would follow me. By the time I entered the hall, I heard him behind me and breathed a sigh of relief.

When Jamal was inside the office with me, I closed the door behind him. He was throwing questions at me before the latch clicked.

"What the fuck is he doing here, Kenya? Does Killian know he's coming here? Does Judy? And who the fuck does he think he is?" Running his hands over his shorn head, he tried to get a grip on himself.

I gave him a minute to do that, and after he'd calmed down enough, I started to answer his questions. "Killian doesn't know he's here. Neither does the High Priestess, I would imagine."

"Then what's he doing here, Kenya?"

"Alex was here with me the other night. The night I felt that... thing...outside. He knew it was here, too, and he called me and told me to get back into the club."

"How did he know?" His tone was suspicious.

"He said he felt it, same as me."

"And he was conveniently keeping an eye out. Just in case? What the hell does he care?"

That was a question I kept asking myself. "I don't know. But he does. Maybe because he was the one who healed me, I don't know," I repeated. "Maybe it's bugging him to find out who or what it was as much as it's bugging us."

"Which leads me back to my original question. What the fuck does he care?"

"I don't have an answer for you," I told him honestly.

He crossed his arms over his chest and stared at me.

"Look," I said. "Isn't it enough to know he's looking out for me? Do we have to know why?"

My answer was a tilt of his head and a raise of one eyebrow.

I sighed heavily. "Look, I really don't know," I told him softly. "I never instigated any contact between us after that night at the swamp house. I swear. It's all on his side."

"Are you sure about that?"

No, no, I wasn't. But if I couldn't sort out my own feelings, how was I supposed to explain them to someone else?

Taking a deep breath through his nose, he exhaled loudly and dropped his arms to his sides. "So, he saved you the other night..."

I nodded. "Apparently, he warded the club. Weeks ago. That's why nothing could get in. I'm safe in here. We're *all* safe in here," I emphasized. "And," I continued, "he warded our house. That same night he walked me home."

Jamal chewed on one corner of his bottom lip while he thought about that. "Well, fuck. I guess I can't kill him now."

"I'd really prefer you didn't."

"Fine," he agreed. "As long as he doesn't come at me again."

"He won't." I reached for his hand and held it between both of mine. "Thank you," I told him earnestly.

"You're welcome," he said, albeit a bit reluctantly. Raising my hand, he dropped a quick kiss on the back of my knuckles, making me smile. It was something he'd been doing since Killian had first brought me into the coven.

As the only female, Jamal had immediately deemed my place as something along the lines of the princess being guarded by her knights. It was silly. But it made me smile.

With one last squeeze, he released my hand. "So, I take it Alex was the one calling you before."

"Yeah."

"Do you know why he's here tonight?"

"I don't. But if you guys would stop trying to kill each other, maybe I could find out."

"Let's do that," he told me, then waved his arm to indicate I was to precede him out the door.

When we got back out to the club, Alex was seated at a table with what appeared to be a glass of whiskey in his hand.

He took one look at Jamal and demanded, "Why is he still here?"

9

ALEX

The male vampire—Jamal—smirked, opening and closing his hands like he was just itching to put them around my throat. However, he was smart enough to do nothing else. I wasn't talking out my ass before when I'd told Kenya he would never be able to get close enough to touch me, and they both knew it.

"He was just leaving," Kenya said.

Her jaw clenched and she shoved her glasses up with a jerky movement when the male crossed his arms over his chest and widened his stance, rooting himself to the spot. "I changed my mind," he told her, although his eyes never left my face. "I think whatever the witch has to tell you can be said in front of me."

"And if what I wanted to tell her was how badly I needed to fuck her right there on that bar?" I told him without missing a beat. "Do you still think that's something that's any of your fucking business, vampire?" The words came out without thought, but once they were said, I realized they weren't far from the truth.

Jamal flashed his fangs but stayed where he was. I had to give him credit for his self-control.

Chancing a glance at Kenya, I found her staring at me with wide eyes. I expected her to be embarrassed, even angry, but she wasn't. Instead, she looked...interested. Turned on, even, by the words I'd blurted out for the shock value, but which were not in the least bit false. "I'm sorry," I told her anyway. "It just came out."

After a moment, she gave me a nod. Then she cleared her throat, trying to be casual about the whole thing. She was wearing the same type of outfit she'd had on last time. Black slacks and heels, only this time she'd paired them with a light purple blouse. Her dark curls were pinned up on top of her head and her black-framed glasses were sliding down her nose.

She was fucking adorable.

And insanely sexy.

As though she suddenly remembered we weren't alone, I watched as she visibly withdrew back into herself. The loss was even more painful than what I'd experienced with the djinn. "Is it back?" she asked. "Is that why you're here?"

So calm. So distant. She was rejecting me before we'd even really gotten to know each other, and it made my chest ache. Was she was only acting this way because the other vampire was here? It was something I would have to find out. "In a way," I told her. Then I laid my cards on the table. "I know who it was."

"You know who tried to kill her?" Jamal asked. "Who was it?"

I got up from the table and went behind the bar, grabbing two more glasses. If he wasn't going to leave, he might as well have a drink with us. "I just found out the other night."

"And you're waiting until now to tell me?" Kenya said, an accusation in her tone.

She was right, and I completely understood how she felt. I'd wanted to come and tell her everything right away, but I was afraid of how she would react. I was still afraid. I'd even contemplated not telling her at all. Except that wasn't fair. She deserved to know the entire truth.

Plus, it gave me an excuse to come and see her.

Putting the whiskey back on the shelf, I slid the two glasses toward them. As though she could tell from my expression she was going to need it, Kenya walked over, took the glass, and downed it. A few seconds later, Jamal did the same, only at a more leisurely pace, taking a seat on a stool.

I raised one eyebrow at Kenya, and she slid her glass back to me. I poured three more glasses and left the bottle on the bar. "His name is Marcus. He's a djinn." That part over, I sipped my whiskey, gearing up for the rest of it.

"Are you fucking kidding me?"

The eerie stillness that came over Jamal was not the reaction I was expecting, but a thousand times more terrifying, if vampires were something I was afraid of.

"A djinn," he repeated in disbelief.

"Yup."

"Why is he after Kenya?"

"I don't know. We didn't get around to the details of that."

"Then how did you know it was this dude that put the curse on her."

I looked him straight in the eye. "Because I know."

"You spoke to him?" Kenya asked.

"I did."

"I don't understand." She slid her glass toward me for another refill. "Did you find him? Did he find you? How did you get him to talk?"

"He found me the other night when I was walking to the High Priestess's house. Confronted me right in the street."

"Was anyone hurt?" she asked. Then her eyes flew to mine as something dawned on her. "Oh, gods, Alex. Were you hurt? Is that why you're only telling me this now?"

A smile teased the corners of my mouth as she searched what she could see of my body for injuries. I should've known that would be the first thing she'd worry about. No questions about why the djinn had come after her. Nothing about whether she was still in danger, only concern for others.

"If you weren't talking about Kenya, what the hell were you talking to a djinn about?"

Ah, the vampire caught on fast. And couldn't give two shits about me or anyone else who wasn't one of his. Maybe we were more alike than I first thought.

I took a breath. Might as well get this part over with. "He claims...he's related to me."

"Wait. What?" Jamal froze with his glass halfway to his lips. He slammed it down onto the counter. "A *djinn* claims he's related to you?"

I nodded, my eyes on Kenya. "He says he's my uncle. Actually my great-great uncle or some shit."

The words were barely out of my mouth when I felt her fear. It hit me in sharp waves, tearing a hole right through my chest. And when I met her eyes, I could see the terror as her swift mind connected the dots. "Kenya..."

She gave a quick shake of her head.

"Would you give us a minute alone?" I asked Jamal, my eyes never leaving her.

"I don't know that that's such a good idea after what you just told us."

His concern was not without justification, but it wasn't necessary. "I just want to talk to Kenya alone. And I will do that one way or the other. So we can do this the easy way and you can walk out of here on your own, or we can do it the hard way and I'll make you leave."

"I don't think the High Priestess will enjoy hearing about that."

"I don't think I give a fuck."

"You will."

Kenya reached over and touched Jamal's arm, but her eyes never left me. "It's okay. Why don't you head home and I'll see you there as soon as we're done here."

He looked like he was going to argue with her, but after a quick glance between the two of us, he sighed heavily. "All right." He covered her hand with his. "Okay. But I'm not going home. I'm just going down the block. I'll wait for you there."

"Okay," she said. "And Jamal," she called as he started to walk away. "Please don't say anything about this to Killian or anyone else. Not just yet."

I didn't think he would agree, but then, with a nod, he walked out the door. Kenya followed him, turning the deadbolt behind him and locking us in.

She didn't turn around right away. I got that. She needed time to get her emotions under control, so I sipped my whiskey as I waited. After a few seconds, she lifted her head and turned to face me, but she still didn't speak.

I came out from behind the bar but didn't go any closer. "You don't have to be afraid of me, Kenya," I told her, but she didn't seem to hear me.

"That's why you were able to remove the curse," she said in a faraway voice. I had the feeling she was talking more to herself than to me. "Because you're just like him."

It was the same conclusion I'd come to myself, but hearing it from her lips...it really made shit real. "No. I'm nothing like him. I use my powers for good. He uses his for evil." I tried a smile, but my joke fell flat. I took a step toward her, my hands out in supplication. "Look, why would I even be here telling you about this if I was going to try to hurt you?"

"To throw me off," she said without pause. "To make me believe you're the good guy."

My arms fell to my sides. "Why the hell would I do that?"

She gave a little shrug, her expression deadpan, but her voice, little more than a whisper, gave away her bewilderment. "I don't know."

"But that's not enough to convince you otherwise."

After a brief hesitation, she shook her head.

However, that tiny sign of indecision gave me hope.

I approached her slowly, giving her plenty of time to tell me to stay the hell away from her, and beyond grateful when she didn't. Slowly, I lifted my hand to her upper arm and let my fingers trail down her silky sleeve. Twining our fingers together, I lifted our joined hands to my mouth and placed a soft kiss on the inside of her wrist.

Her lips parted on an intake of breath and her pulse sped up beneath my lips. Placing her hand flat against my chest, I stood absolutely still and reached out with everything I was, wrapping my very soul around her. I knew she sensed it when her wide eyes flew to mine. "I know you can feel me," I told her. "Do I feel like something you need to be afraid of?"

"Yes," she whispered.

The answer surprised me and caused me more pain than I was expecting to feel. "I don't want you to be afraid of me."

"What *do* you want from me, Alex?"

I knew the answer to that, but I didn't know if she was ready to hear it. So, I said nothing.

Gods, she was so beautiful, looking up at me, her brown eyes wary behind the lenses of her glasses, her chest rising and falling with unsteady breaths. Images filled my head of this woman naked in my bed, her mahogany skin silky and warm beneath my hands and mouth. Dark nipples tipping the breasts I desperately wanted to feel pressed against my chest. Her full thighs spread wide so I could see how wet she was. How much she wanted me, too.

Something in my expression must've given away my thoughts, or maybe she'd forgotten her promise to stay out of my head, for I heard her breath catch in a quick inhale. And her eyes, so dark and mistrustful a moment before, began to burn bright with the same fire that was heating my blood.

The tip of her tongue wet her bottom lip, and I was lost.

10

KENYA

Oh gods, what was happening?

Alex stared down at me, his eyes tracking every tiny movement I made. I was used to this kind of thing from vampires, whose senses were in overdrive and tended to pick up on stuff humans wouldn't notice.

But I'd never before been hit with this level of intensity from someone who wasn't one of us. The way he was looking at me made me wonder if this was how humans felt when they stared into our eyes and we bewitched them with our vampire mind games.

Yet, it wasn't just his gaze holding me captive. His magic surrounded me...No. It was more than that. It was like his life force had left his body and everything that was Alex was now wrapped around me, like the spirit in those Anne Rice novels I read years ago.

Or like a lover.

I took a shuddering breath, and his scent filled my nose, coating the back of my throat and making my mouth water. His blood was the most delicious thing I'd ever smelled, only slightly muted by the body wash he showered with. I'd noticed this before, and I'd had to do everything in my power not to show this weakness to him.

But right now, the urge to lick the side of his throat so I could feel the pulse throbbing beneath my tongue was near overwhelming. My gums burned as my fangs elongated, aching to pierce through his skin to the warm blood beneath. My eyes fell from his perfect lips to the side of his throat, just beneath his hard jawline.

"Do it," he told me in a husky voice.

Gods, I wanted to. Just a little taste…

"Go on, Kenya. It's okay. Do it."

With a helpless sound I couldn't control, I stepped into him, his strong arms coming around me as he lowered his head to mine, his jaw rough against my cheek. My hands fisted in his coat and I did what I'd wanted to do for so long, flicking my tongue out quickly, tasting the salt of his tan skin before I ran it slowly along his pulse. It beat strong and steady, unlike my own, which was racing like I'd just outrun a pack of werewolves. Unable to resist, I scraped one fang over his skin, feeling his heartbeat with the sensitive tip but not breaking the skin.

Alex sucked in a breath and moaned as a shudder ran through his big body, and I felt an answering need low in my groin.

I'd never fed from a warlock before, and the thought frightened me. What would happen? Was the magic there in his blood? How would it affect me?

The thought sobered me instantly and I pulled away from the temptation of his throat before I did something I would regret. Witches were strictly forbidden to us. Well, at least they were before Killian mated with Lizzy. However, I had no idea what that meant for the rest of us; if it changed anything within our agreement with them or not. Without knowing for sure, I couldn't take the chance. And besides, it wasn't like I could feed from him and then wipe his memory like we did to the humans that came into the club. Witches weren't so easily manipulated.

But before I could step completely out of his embrace, he caught me by the back of my neck and pulled my mouth to his.

His kiss was hard. Hungry. Like he wanted to devour me the only way he could. And he knew exactly how to do it, teasing my fangs with his tongue and nipping at my lips. My response was just as urgent, the lust for his blood swiftly changing to a starving hunger for his body. He tasted like whiskey and smelled like dark, honeyed wine, and I wanted him inside of me in every possible way.

Shoving his coat off his broad shoulders and down his arms, I let it fall to the floor and shoved him into the wall behind him.

He grunted when he hit, and I was worried I'd been too rough in my haste to feel him closer to me. His hands and mouth never stopped though, yanking my shirt out from my pants and sliding beneath it, his palms warm and rough on the bare skin of my back.

Oh gods.

His mouth left mine and I cried out in protest, only to moan a second later when I felt him kissing the side of my neck, his mouth hot and wet against my skin. He continued down, sinking his teeth into the muscle between my neck and shoulder before soothing the bite with more kisses.

I gripped his shoulders, my legs like Jell-O and my head thrown back to allow him access, my fangs on full display. One of his hands slid down to my ass, lifting my hips into his until I felt his hard length pressing into me.

"Kenya..."

My name was little more than a ragged gasp. And then his lips were back on mine, one hand gripping my neck and the other my ass, his hips rolling against mine. I forgot to be careful with my fangs. I forgot everything but the things this man was making me feel.

I wanted more.

The world spun around me and I felt the wall against my back, Alex now pressing into me, pulling one of my legs up around his hip until I could feel his hardness between my thighs. His other hand was back under my blouse, burning my skin, squeezing my breast, then pinching the nipple through my bra.

And through all of that, he was kissing me like his life depended on it, and all I could do was hold on for dear life as he consumed me. He was all I could see. All I could hear. All I could feel. The rush of blood—both his and mine—filled my ears and his scent filled my nose. It was a disconcerting feeling for one who was used to being the predator, not the prey.

But it wasn't just his physical form possessing me. His shields were down completely. I heard his desperate need and felt his power swirling around me, holding me to him tighter than his strong arms.

The scents, the sounds, the magic...it was too much. I pressed my hands against his hard chest. "Alex, stop," I whispered against his mouth. "Stop."

Immediately, he stilled, kissing my bruised lips softly a few times before pressing his forehead to mine. We stayed like that for quite a while, our heaving breaths mingling as our pulses slowed. "I'm sorry," I began.

"No. No. Don't apologize. You don't have to apologize," he insisted. His voice was rough. Raw. "I should be the one doing that. I got carried away." He exhaled and removed his hand from beneath my shirt as I lowered my leg. Then he stepped back just enough to put some space between us.

I shivered, wrapping my arms around myself, the air cold and impersonal against my skin as we stared at one another. I already missed his heat, and my throat burned with thirst. But I couldn't go there. We couldn't go there. Desperate for one last memory, I reached out to him with my mind, but his shields were back in place. That loss of connection froze me out more than the physical space between us, and I mourned its loss even as I knew he was right to do it. "We can't do this," I reminded myself aloud. "It's against the rules. You shouldn't even be here."

"Do you want me to leave?"

I met the challenge in his eyes and told him the truth. "No. But you have to. And we can't tell anyone about what just happened."

"What about Jamal?"

"What about him?"

"Won't he smell me on you?"

Shit. He was right. "I have a change of clothes in the back. I'll wash up and change."

I saw the question in his eyes.

"Sometimes things get a little messy in the private room."

Understanding dawned across his face, followed swiftly by the angry set of his jaw.

"Really?" I asked him when I noticed his expression. "You know what I am, Alex. What we do here. As a matter of fact, I believe it was your aunt who insisted we keep things contained within The Quarter and specifically this club. So, don't look at me like that when I'm up front with you about why we need to keep a change of clothes here. No one dies. Everyone has a good time. Me and mine are fed. No harm done."

"It's not that," he told me.

"Then what is it?"

But he just shook his head. However, he still stared at me, his fists clenched at his sides.

"What?" I insisted.

I didn't think he was going to answer me at first, and I was about to walk away when he said, "I don't like the idea of you being that...intimate with someone."

Well, well, color me surprised. That's not what I was expecting. "I have to feed, Alex." I didn't bother telling him that I only did so when the thirst was near unbearable. That I didn't take advantage of what I was now.

He looked away, scrubbing his face with his hands. When he met my eyes again, his were still not happy, but they were resigned. "I know."

There was more he wanted to say, I could tell by the look on his face, but he held himself back. Even his power was held tightly, wrapped around him like a second skin and no longer holding me in its grasp.

My anger melted away, replaced once again by the loneliness that had assaulted me since the first night he came to see me. And he hadn't even left yet. I dropped my eyes, not wanting him to notice the longing I felt for him. Clearing my throat, I made to move past him, and after a brief pause, he stepped away and let me pass. I tried to remember everything from our earlier conversation before we'd gotten...sidetracked. "Is there anything else I need to know about the djinn?" I asked him as I got my coat and bag from behind the bar.

"No."

Slinging the strap of my bag over my shoulder and folding my coat over my arms, I stared at him from a safer distance. "Is there anything else I need to know about you?"

He stayed where he was, but I felt his essence touch me, timidly at first, and then with slightly more force before it retracted again. "Only that you don't need to be frightened of me, Kenya. I would never, ever, hurt you."

Why did I have the feeling he was talking about more than the fact that he was part djinn?

He was waiting for a response, but I wasn't sure what to say, so I just gave him a nod. "I need to go home and figure out how I'm going to let Killian know you told us tonight without actually telling him you were the one who told us."

"Don't you need to change your clothes first?"

Shit. "Yes. Thank you." I laid my bag and my coat on top of the bar, then made my way back out to the floor, stopping near the door. "Um…"

Saving me from my awkwardness, he grabbed his coat from the floor, pausing when he reached me. "Lock the door behind me."

I trembled when he brushed my cheek with the back of his knuckles, then gently pushed my glasses back into place.

"I'm leaving, but I won't be gone. If you need me for anything, I'll be here." Ducking his head, he dropped a quick kiss on my lips and walked out the door.

Sorrow mixed with relief as I locked the door behind him. Knowing what he was, I doubted I would ever feel safe around him. Aroused? Hell, yes. But safe?

My instincts told me I was right to fear him.

And my instincts were never wrong.

11

ALEX

When I stepped outside, I saw Jamal leaning against a streetlight just down the block. He didn't move. Didn't wave. He just stared at me.

Pulling my coat up to protect the back of my neck from the chill, I turned my back to him and headed in the opposite direction. I didn't rush, knowing he'd stay there to watch me go, and giving Kenya time to get changed. Plus, it would piss him off.

And that was just fun for me.

I licked my bottom lip. I could still taste Kenya on my mouth. Could still smell her on my clothes. Jamal was upwind from me, which was a stroke of luck on my part. Something told me he would've been on me by now if he'd caught the slightest whiff of what we'd been up to in there.

And thank the gods for the wonderful people of The Quarter who kept the party going until the wee hours of the morning. With all of the jazz and the chatter of tourists, I doubted even he could've heard us from that far away.

I kept everything all calm and cool until I finally turned a corner. It was only then that I allowed my frustration to show. Raking my fingers through my hair, I quickened my pace.

I wasn't ready to leave her.

But I couldn't have stayed, not when she was clearly so uncomfortable by me being there.

Fuck, maybe I shouldn't have told her anything. At least not the part about me. But I couldn't just let her run around New Orleans without knowing the danger she was in. And what if she found out some other way? Then I'd not only be part djinn, I'd have lived up to the reputation of one. I'd be a liar. Someone she couldn't trust.

As I neared the end of The Quarter, the crowd—for what it was this time of year—began to thin out, awarding me a clear view of the High Priestess of my coven waiting for me across the street, just on the other side of the border drawn by our pact with the vampires. She looked like anyone's elderly aunt in her puffed up coat and sturdy shoes. Her short, gray hair was still peppered with the original black, and her bright blue eyes were unclouded by age.

Walking up to her, I didn't try to make excuses or explain my way out of anything. She knew exactly why I was wandering around The Quarter, and I wasn't going to insult her intelligence or mine by pretending otherwise. Plus, she was my mother's sister, and it would be disrespectful of my mother's memory. "Hey," I greeted her.

"Hey yourself," she said.

She came to walk beside me, and we headed in the direction of the garden district. She didn't say anything else for almost a block, and I imagined she was getting her thoughts together. I enjoyed the peace while it lasted. I loved my aunt, and I knew she loved me, but as the head witch of our coven, she sometimes enjoyed the rank of her position a little too much.

However, when she did finally start talking, it wasn't at all what I'd expected.

"He's here, isn't he? The djinn." She kept her voice down to barely above a whisper.

"Yes."

She made an affirmative. "I thought I felt something." She glanced over at me. "Has he approached you?"

"Yes."

She nodded thoughtfully. "What did he tell you, Alex?"

"That he was my uncle. Well," I amended. "My great-great uncle, I believe is what he said."

She glanced over at me. "I'm sorry I didn't tell you. Didn't warn you. You *and* your sister. I should have, and that's on me."

"You've known all this time?" My voice was full of all of the disbelief and betrayal I was feeling.

"I did," she told me. "And I should have told you," she repeated.

"Why didn't you?" I noticed we were heading to her house, not my apartment.

"I don't know," she said. "I guess because I was hoping he wouldn't find us. Or that he wouldn't care enough to."

"So, it's true?" I asked her after a pause. "He is my uncle?" Even though I felt the djinn was telling me the truth when he'd told me, I still wanted the confirmation of someone I trusted.

"It's true," she told me.

My next inhale was shaky. I'd been sitting on this info for a few days now, and I'd known there was something different about me and Alice, but somehow it hadn't seemed real until just this very moment. I'd hoped there was some kind of reasonable explanation. "Well...fuck."

"I really am sorry," she told me. "For not telling you."

I didn't respond. Yeah, she should've fucking said something. She'd had plenty of chances, especially after our mother died. But I could understand why she didn't.

"So, what did he say to you other than to tell you who he is?"

"He wants me and Alice to come north with him."

It was a few seconds before she could ask, "And what are you both going to do?"

I frowned as I glanced over at her. "What do you mean? Am I going with him?"

She nodded.

I opened my mouth to ask her how she could even think that I would do such a thing, but then I snapped it shut again. I'd never really considered what it would mean for me to take him up on his offer because I couldn't see past the fact that he'd tried to kill Kenya. I still didn't see how I could ever willingly be anywhere near that guy. That he was family didn't mean shit to me.

But I hadn't thought about the fact that he was the only one who shared this power I had inside of me. That Alice had inside of her. Which meant he was the only one who could teach us how to control it. How to use it. How to live with it. "I don't know," I told her in all honesty. "I hadn't thought about it until just now. I haven't even told Alice yet."

"Because you're too worried about Kenya," she stated.

"Yes," I told her.

We walked in silence for another few minutes. Then she asked, "Do the vampires know you broke our pact by encroaching on their territory?"

I scoffed at her choice of words. "I wasn't encroaching."

"You were in The Quarter, which is the safe zone allotted to them in our pact. The Garden District is ours. Unless permission is granted by the other party, we are to stay within our own territories or the neutral zone in between. Did you have permission from the vampires? From Killian?"

"No," I admitted. "I did not."

"Then you were, indeed, encroaching." Though she scolded me, her blue eyes were filled with concern. "And how is Kenya?"

Beautiful. Intelligent. Sexy. Innocent and sultry all at the same time. Scared to death of me. "She's good."

We reached her house and stopped at the foot of the driveway that ran alongside. "Would you like some tea?"

This was her way of saying the conversation wasn't finished, so we might as well go in where it's warm. I glanced up at the one-story house, small and compact, but with four white columns holding up the roof over the front porch. In the dark, with the gathering fog coming off the water and the low-hanging tree covering one corner of the front yard, it all looked a little old and creepy, even though it was a newer home. But I knew inside it would be light and bright. And if I refused, we would stand right out here on the sidewalk until she got what she wanted to know. "Sure. Thanks."

She nodded, pleased I'd made the right choice and headed up the drive around the house to the back door. She opened it without a key and walked into her white kitchen, flicking on lights and calling to her cat, Ted Danson, that she was home.

Ted, a gray tabby with the same blue eyes as the actor he was named after, looked up from his place on the back of the couch, flicked his tail in greeting, and went back to watching whatever had caught his interest out the side window.

Judy filled the tea kettle and set it on the stove to heat. While she did that, I took off my coat, laid it over the back of one of the kitchen chairs, and made myself at home.

When she turned around and saw me sitting there, she smiled. "It's been a while since you've come over."

She was right. It had been. "I'm sorry," I told her earnestly. "I've been preoccupied."

"Yes, let's talk about that." Getting two cups down from the cabinet, she readied the tea bags and set them on the counter until the water boiled. Then she joined me at the table.

"I'd like to know about my father," I told her before she could start bombarding me with more questions.

"I never met him."

I stilled. "Marcus told me he's the descendent of the daughter of his brother. But I'd still like to know about him. Mom would never tell us anything."

The kettle whistled and Judy got up to get our tea. "Honestly, I don't know much about him either, other than the fact that he broke your mother's heart." I waited for her to come back to the table and sit down before I asked her to go on, but she only said, "I'm sorry, honey. Your mom showed up here shortly after me and Lizzy's mom came down here from Washington. She was in tears and pregnant with you and your sister. She wouldn't talk about it much, and at first we were scared that something terrible had happened to our sister after we'd abandoned her on that damn mountain. But, after a while, we figured out that wasn't the case at all. She was heartbroken though, until you two were born."

"So, no one knows anything about him?"

"Not that I know of. But that brings me around to the part of the story I wanted to tell you about. Which is the reason we left our home and moved way down here to Louisiana."

I'd already guessed. "Marcus."

She nodded, then sipped at her tea. "He came back. This was in the early 1980s. He killed your great-grandparents and took over the coven. Shortly after, a large group of us escaped, scattering all over the world. Your mom didn't want to come with us, and I didn't understand why at first, until she showed up here in the condition she was in."

"Why did you pick New Orleans?" I asked out of curiosity.

She shrugged. "Oh, I don't know. I always had a thing for Cajun food, so there was that. And, at the time, I figured there wasn't much chance of vampires settling here what with the hot summers and sunshine and that." She laughed quietly. "Imagine my surprise to find them already here when we got here."

"It's not the 1800s anymore," I teased her. "We have technology now."

"Oh, hush." Her mouth twisted and she rolled her eyes as I laughed. Listening to me, she got serious again. "I haven't heard you laugh like that in a long time."

She was right. For the last few years, I'd felt more angry than joyful. But I was beginning to wonder if it wasn't anger at all, but just me trying to deal with this shit inside of me that had finally grown tired of lying dormant. At least, it had been until I'd shoved it into Kenya to remove the curse. "I don't know what I'm supposed to do now," I admitted.

Judy's eyes met mine. "I think you've done all you can, honey. I imagine the reason you were in The Quarter tonight was to warn Kenya about Marcus?"

I nodded.

"And did she believe you?"

"Yeah, she believed me. But that's not what I was talking about."

She sat up in her chair and wrapped her hands around her cup. "Oh. That."

I leaned forward, setting my own rapidly cooling tea to the side. "Tell me what I should do," I pleaded. Because I honestly didn't know. I felt like I was standing at the end of a road that veered off in two different directions, and I had no idea which fork I should choose because either one of them would take me away from this life I knew now, one way or the other.

"The first thing you need to do is stay away from the vampires, Alex."

"I don't think I can do that."

"You must. If Killian catches you sniffing around Kenya—"

"I'm not 'sniffing around' her," I argued. "I'm trying to save her life."

"You already did that."

"And yet, he came back."

She sat back, studying me. However, I could tell she wasn't seeing me at all. "I don't think he's after her at all," she finally said. "And we don't know that it was him who tried to kill her in the first place."

"It was him," I told her.

"You can't know that."

I shook my head. She was wrong. I did know that. "Who the hell else would it have been? Unless there are djinn just running amok in this world and nobody bothered to tell any of us?"

I waited for her to say that was exactly what was happening, but she didn't. "No," she said.

"I felt him, Aunt Jude. When I was inside of Kenya, I felt the magic...the, the...the *power*. And I felt that same power when he confronted me. The exact same thing. It was him. I'm absolutely positive about that."

She stared down at the table, her forehead wrinkled in thought. "I just don't get it, though. Why would he go after someone like Kenya?"

"I don't know. But I won't let him get to her again." I paused, waiting for her to look at me. "I *can't*," I emphasized. "Do you understand?"

My aunt's blue eyes were sharp, her expression anguished. "Oh, Alex."

12

KENYA

I was standing behind the bar, my eyes on Brogan, who was down to almost nothing but his unbuttoned Hawaiian shirt and tiny G-string.

He really had a thing for those shirts. And as far as I knew, he'd never been to Hawaii.

We had a full house tonight, and he was showing them one hell of a good time, which meant no one was asking for drinks. Instead, they were all surrounding the stage, pushing each other out of the way to stick their hard-earned dollars down their bras for him to fetch with his teeth. Just one of the many things Brogan was known for.

But my mind was far away from The Purple Fang and my good-looking friend stripping on stage. Entirely too far.

Wandering away to things it really shouldn't be thinking about at all.

Actually, just one "thing" in particular.

I couldn't sort out how I felt about Alex. I was having a hard time reconciling the fact that the same man who was so caring and protective, the man who could kiss me senseless and make my blood burn in my veins, was from the same breed as the thing that had tried to kill me. Fear and desire warred within me, unable to come to any kind of balance, and it was making me itch.

Though we were all familiar with each other, the vampires and the witches, something had happened that night he'd saved me from the curse. Something I couldn't explain. I felt linked to him now somehow. I missed him when he wasn't around—the sound of his voice, the quirk of his lips, the smell of his blood. And the more time that passed, the more I watched the door, hoping he would walk in, even though I knew it was ridiculous to expect him to just come waltzing into the club, like he wasn't a warlock and I, a vampire.

But in that same vein, I also knew I couldn't trust him.

As though he somehow knew I was thinking about him, my phone buzzed in my back pocket. I pulled it out and saw that I had a text from a number with no name. A number I was coming to recognize. My heart sped up as I swiped open my screen.

Hey.

I glanced up at Brogan, who was flashing his "fake" fangs and humping a lucky guest who'd paid to get into the "Bite Me" chair on stage (another $20 and she'd get a private bite in the back room), then toward the back office where Killian was talking to Dae-Jung. The office door was closed. I hadn't told him yet that we knew who it was who had cursed me. I planned to do it tonight after closing time.

When I looked down, there was another text.

I lied to you. I'm not sorry at all.

Heat crawled up my chest and throat. I knew exactly what he was talking about.

I want to see you.

I shook my head, realized Alex couldn't see me, and tapped out a quick reply.

We can't.

As much as a part of me wanted to see him, a shiver ran up my spine when I remembered how it felt to have his sorcery wrapped around me. I couldn't forget that Alex was part djinn, and there would always be that part of him that I would never be able to feel comfortable around.

But he was not to be so easily deterred.

Meet me at St. Louis #1. I'll wait for you.

I really couldn't. We'd just be asking for trouble...

I just want to talk.

I snorted out loud at that one. Famous last words if I'd ever heard them. Glancing around, I saw Brogan—in nothing but his G-string now, muscular ass flexing with every step—leading the lucky lady off the stage and toward the back room, a wad of cash in her hand. Dae came out from the back right on time, jogging toward the stage in tight blue jeans and a white tank top as the music changed. It was only the two of them tonight, Jamal and Elias had the night off. And Killian didn't dance as much now that he had Lizzy.

As Dae was getting into position, women rushed the bar, eager to refill their glasses before he got to "the good part."

Fine, I responded, then put my phone back into my pocket.

I smiled at my first customer, getting her order and the woman's next to her. Careful to stay at human speed, I filled mugs and mixed shots. I didn't allow myself to think too much about what I'd just agreed to. But maybe I should text Jamal and let him know where I would be, just in case.

As I worked on my last order of the rush, I looked up to find Killian watching me from the office doorway with a strange expression on his face. I felt a nervous flutter in my stomach, but quickly quashed it. There was no reason for it. There's no way he could know about my conversation with Alex. Maybe I'd just forgotten where I was for a second and had done something that could've tipped off a customer that we weren't exactly the type of club they really wanted to frequent.

I gave him a little wave, finished the drink I was working on, gave it to the customer, and rang it up on her tab. When I looked over again, Killian was gone.

Quickly, I pulled out my phone and deleted our messages, feeling like a teenage girl who'd been caught texting the boy from the wrong side of the tracks. The one her father had forbidden her to see. However, my situation was a hell of a lot more serious than that. If caught, it wasn't like I'd get grounded to my room for the weekend with my phone taken away. I was no young girl, and this wasn't your ordinary forbidden romance.

No, if it was discovered Alex and I had been meeting secretly, it could cause a war between his people and mine. A war some may not survive if tempers became heated.

I wondered if the mating between Killian and Lizzy might eventually change things, especially now that Lizzy was actually taking part in the witch's coven, unlike when she'd first arrived in the city. Even hosting meetings in her voodoo shop that she ran strictly for tourists—Ancient Magicks. She didn't talk about witch business much to Killian, and not at all to anyone else in our house. I had to respect her for that. It couldn't be easy dividing your loyalties between your aunt—the High Priestess—and your mate.

But nothing had been officially decided that I knew of. Not that it mattered. Alex had always had something edgy about him. And now, knowing what he was…well, it frightened me, if I were to be honest with myself. And I'd had enough of that in my human life, being tossed from one foster home to the next, never knowing if the people who were supposed to care for me would love me or beat me. If I was really lucky, they collected the money for my care and ignored me completely.

Until Killian found me.

I sighed. It's not that I perceived myself to be a weak female. I didn't. I wasn't. Especially not now. For the sake of the gods, I was a vampire, albeit not a very good one. Not many things could harm me. But I now had a family that consisted of five overprotective brothers and a new sister-in-law. I had consistency in my life. I had security. We even had an old dog to love, thanks to Lizzy. And all of that was not something I ever wanted to give up.

Yeah. Alex and I definitely needed to talk.

The rest of the night passed by with little fanfare. Killian left right after last call, only stopping by the bar to tell me he was heading out. Brogan was back on the stage entertaining what remained of the crowd. And Dae was in the back room having his dinner.

I made sure the bar was clean and stocked for the following night, turned off the open sign, and locked the door before I went back to the office to tally up the cash. The guys would let the last, lingering customers out when they were done with them.

From the corner of my eye, I noticed a brunette woman in a red dress that matched her lipstick sitting to one side of the stage. She appeared to be finishing her drink. But her eyes weren't on Brogan, they were on the curtain that blocked the customer's view from the private performances that happened there, where Dae was now feeding.

It seemed like I'd seen her here before tonight. Maybe she was a local? Not the majority of our clientele, but not unheard of. We just had to be more careful around those customers. They tended to be less enthusiastic with their alcohol than the tourists, and therefore not as easily swayed. With a mental shrug, I took the cashbox into the office and locked the door behind me.

I was just finishing up when Brogan knocked on the door. "Hey, girl. You about ready?"

Shit. I forgot about my nightly escorts. Ever since the night I'd told Killian about the djinn lurking around outside—not knowing what it was at the time—he had added his orders to Alex's (unbeknownst to him) that I wasn't to be on the streets alone.

I needed to get rid of Brogan, but how?

The answer came in the form of the brunette woman. She was standing just down the block from the club when we came out, her red dress covered with a black, leather jacket. But what was weird? She stood right in the middle of the sidewalk, brazen as could be, not trying at all to be inconspicuous.

"Fuck me," Brogan muttered as I locked the door.

I glanced over at the woman again. "What does she want?" I asked him. I wasn't overly concerned. It wasn't the first time a customer had waited outside for us to close and the dancers to come out. And anyway, I had my own problem waiting for me to worry about.

"Not what you think," he told me.

"Do you need to go handle that?"

He glanced down at me. "No. I'm supposed to stay with you. She can wait."

We started walking in the opposite direction toward the house. I was thinking I'd just have to let him walk me home and then sneak out when I noticed him looking back over his shoulder. I did the same.

The woman was still there. Same spot. Hadn't moved an inch.

I looked up at Brogan and saw his jaw clench. "Brogan, really. If you need to go handle that, go ahead. The house is only a few blocks away and there's still quite a few people out tonight. I'll be okay."

He just shook his head without looking at me.

"Look," I told him. "I'll call Jamal. Have him meet me along the way."

I saw a hint of uncertainty in his green eyes, but he finally agreed. "I won't be long."

"It's okay. Go take care of...whatever you need to take care of." I smiled and pulled my phone out of my pocket, acting like I was getting ready to text Jamal.

"All right." Wrapping one large hand around the side of my head, he pulled me toward him and dropped a kiss on the top of my head. "Be careful."

"Will do," I promised, and watched him walk away without a backward glance.

My heart began to pound, and my mouth went dry with that strange mixture of fear and excitement I felt every time Alex was anywhere near me. At least now I knew why.

The closer I drew to Basin Street where the cemetery was located, the faster my steps became, even as my mind screamed at me to turn around, to go home, to tell him this was a bad idea and that he needed to stay away from me. And really mean it this time.

But it wasn't until the stone wall that surrounded the cemetery appeared that I hesitated at all.

What the hell am I doing?

With a quick glance around, I continued down St. Louis Street. There was an apartment building across from the cemetery, and just past the apartments was a parking lot. I waited until I was to the lot before, with one last look around, I easily leapt the wall and landed in a crouch on the other side. The cemetery was dark, the aboveground tombs casting long shadows in the faint light of the streetlights.

Due to the famous graves within, the cemetery had been subject to a lot of vandalism over the years, and so the city finally closed it to the public except for guided tours. Why humans always had to ruin everything, I would never know. However, this suited our purpose tonight just fine. And as I spotted Alex standing next to an impressive tomb with a cross on the top near the center of the graveyard, I was glad there was no one there to see how I stopped and stared.

His feet were braced apart, his hands in the front pockets of his jeans, his coat open, and his eyes on the ground in front of him.

He appeared lost in thought and hadn't seen me yet. As I watched, he gave his head a little shake, like he was shaking away ugly thoughts, and pulled out his phone and checked the screen, then shoved it back into his pocket.

I wondered how long he'd been waiting for me. And as I watched him, I couldn't fight the response I had to his nearness. His scent came to me on the breeze, and I closed my eyes briefly as the bloodlust hit me hard, my fangs shooting down before it spiraled through me, mixing with my hunger to feel his hardness against me, his mouth on mine and his hands on my skin. Desire clenched the muscles deep in my womb, so sharp I gasped out loud.

His head suddenly lifted and snapped around, his eyes pegging me where I stood. In the darkness, they glowed a dark gold for a moment before they dimmed, blending into the shadows of his features.

Pulling his hands from his pockets, he started walking toward me and I did the same, meeting him somewhere in the middle. I wasn't sure what I expected. That he would grab me in his arms and kiss me senseless? Or at the very least, greet me in some manner that told me he'd missed me.

But he didn't do any of that. He drew to a stop just out of my reach. Taking his cue, I stopped also.

His eyes grew hard as they travelled over my face. "You're afraid."

I took a steadying breath. He was right. Beneath my need for him was still a lingering fear. "I am."

His expression never changed, but I heard the hesitation in his voice when he asked, "Do you want to leave?"

I thought about that for a long, hard moment. Then I shook my head.

"No."

13

ALEX

The sense of relief that hit me was so strong I grew lightheaded. "Good," I told her.

She came to stand in front of me, and I couldn't stop myself from running my eyes over her. She was so fucking gorgeous with her hair in soft curls and her curves complimented by form-fitted dress pants and a tapered jacket.

"You said you wanted to talk," she reminded me.

I almost laughed out loud. *Talk.* Yeah, I'd said that. I'd even meant it at the time. But now that she was here, so close to me, all I could think about was kissing her again. "How are you?" I asked.

"I'm fine," she told me.

Fine. Any man worth his salt knew what that actually meant. She wasn't fine at all.

She was nervous. Jumpy. It made me want to take her in my arms and kiss her until she was making those little noises deep in her throat and her fangs were bared with lust. I wanted to feel her sink those fangs into my throat, or anywhere else she wanted to bite me, for that matter. I wanted to give her pleasure. Give her life.

I...*hungered* for her. It was like nothing I'd ever felt before. And from the way the tips of her fangs peeked out from beneath her full upper lip when she spoke, she felt the same about me.

I racked my brain for something to discuss, something that would make me sound somewhat intelligent, rather than the jumble of raw emotions I really was whenever she was anywhere near me.

"I think this was a mistake," she suddenly whispered. Fast as a whip, she turned to leave.

But I was faster, appearing in front of her before she could run off.

Kenya pulled up short with a gasp. "How do you do that?"

"What?" I asked, distracted by the sight of her close up and personal. Gods, she was beautiful. Her skin smooth. Her eyes bright. In the dark, I could see different shades of browns and greens and golds, the vampire she was lighting her up from the inside out.

"How do you move so fast, Alex? You move as fast as I do. Something no human, not even a witch, should be able to do."

Oh. That. "I don't really know," I answered honestly. "I've always been able to do it."

She stared at me for a long time, her hands fisted at her sides. "It's the djinn inside of you."

"Perhaps." It could possibly explain many things about myself, about my magic. But I didn't want to talk about that. I didn't even want to think about it right now. "Please don't be frightened of me, Kenya. I'm still the same guy."

"No," she said. "No, Alex. You're not." She paused, looking away for a moment before she brought her attention back to me. "This isn't a good idea. I shouldn't have come."

"Stop saying that." The words came out harsher than I'd intended, and I made an effort to get a grip on the whirlwind of emotions slamming around inside of me, forcing myself to relax and not frighten her more.

"Alex, I can't keep doing this. Someone is going to find out about us. They'll pull you from my head when I'm not paying attention, and then the secret will be out—"

"So, let it be out."

She snapped her mouth shut. "We can't do that."

"Why? Why don't we just tell them, Kenya?"

"Tell them what, exactly?"

I opened my mouth to speak, and then shut it again, thinking carefully about my words before I said them. "Tell them that we're friends."

She studied me above the rim of her glasses. "Is that what we are, Alex? Friends?"

"No," I told her.

My honesty seemed to surprise her. Unable to stand the distance between us anymore, I reached out and took her hand, lacing my fingers through hers. Her hands were graceful, slender, so fragile feeling, even though they could crush my skull with very little effort on her part. "Come here." She let me lead her between two large graves. Two smaller tombs stood between them, providing us a secluded area of sorts. I didn't like having to hide, and honestly, I was tired of it. But I thought it would make her more comfortable to not be right out in the open.

Tucking her into the corner, I brushed a stray curl from her face.

She swallowed visibly. "Alex." There was an admonishment in her tone, and I smiled.

"Don't look at me like that," I told her. "I just couldn't stand you being so far away and looking at me the way you were."

"Looking at you in what way?"

"Like I'm some sort of monster," I told her softly.

Her expression softened. "I didn't mean to."

"I know." I forced myself to back off and leaned against the tomb beside her. "I want to kiss you," I told her. "I won't if you don't want me to, but I just wanted you to know what's going through my head right now."

"What else is going through your head?" she asked softly.

"Do you really want to know?"

"Yes."

I stared out at the cemetery. All of those dead souls. The bodies decaying until they were nothing but ash, ready to be brushed aside when the time came to make room for the mortal body of the next family member. "Tell me about your life," I said. "Before you were a vampire."

She turned her head to look at me. It wasn't what she'd expected me to ask. But if she was going to shut me down, I couldn't keep talking about all of the things I wanted to do to her. What I wanted her to do to me. Not if I wanted to retain any kind of self-control.

"Um, what do you want to know?"

I turned toward her, crossing my arms over my chest and propping my shoulder against the tomb. "Everything," I told her. "Tell me everything. What's your full name? When were you born?"

"Darce," she said after a pause. "My last name is Darce."

"And when were you born Kenya Darce?"

"Sometime in the 1960s. I'm not sure exactly. I was given up by my birthparents."

"Mmm...not as old as I thought."

"Are you saying I look old?" she demanded. But then she smiled. It was a ridiculous question and she knew it, as vampires didn't physically age past the year they were when they were turned.

She dazzled me. It was the only way to describe it. "So, you were adopted by a family?" I asked when I could speak again.

She looked down at her hands, twisted together nervously in front of her. "No. I went into the foster system. I never knew what family was until Killian found me."

In those few simple sentences about her past, she had just explained so much to me. I could also tell it pained her to speak of it. "I'd heard that Killian never turned anyone who wasn't already dying. Is that true?"

She visibly relaxed, and I could tell she was relieved to be off the subject of her upbringing. Someday, I would ask her to tell me more. But not tonight. "Yes. And even then, he asked all of us if it was what we wanted first. Well," she pushed her glasses up on her nose, "all except Jamal. He was the first vampire Killian turned."

I could tell by the way she frowned and glanced away this was another sensitive subject, so I didn't pry anymore.

"How are you doing?" she asked. "Since finding out."

There was no need for her to elaborate, I knew exactly what she was talking about. "I don't really know," I admitted. "Part of me is relieved to know why I've always felt different than the rest of my family. And part of me is absolutely horrified and scared to death I might accidentally hurt someone I love."

"Alex—"

I cut her off. "I can feel it growing within me, Kenya. Like it was just lying there dormant until that night at the swamp house. Strange, don't you think?" I glanced up at her, but I couldn't take the look of sympathy on her face, so looked away again. "Hell, I'm in my thirties. Why is that side of me just now making itself known?" I shoved my hand through my short hair.

Kenya was quiet for a long time. "Is he still around? The djinn?"

"Yes. I can still feel him." Like a storm cloud hovering over the city. "But it's okay. It's safe for us to be here right now. He's nowhere close."

"How do you know that?"

"I just do," I told her. Pushing myself off the tomb, I came around to stand in front of her. I didn't want to think about Marcus. "I'm still thinking about kissing you."

Slowly, her hands came up between us and she flattened her palms on my chest. I closed my eyes, her touch burning through the thin cotton shirt I wore. I waited for her to push me away, but she didn't.

"You said you wanted to talk," she reminded me.

Lowering my head, I ran my nose along her hairline near her temple. Her hair smelled like coconut and some kind of sweet spice I couldn't name. "I am talking. I'm talking about how much I want to kiss you."

I felt her turn her face into my neck. "You smell so good," she breathed.

My body hardened at her words. She'd spoken so quietly, I don't think she'd meant for me to hear her. But I answered her anyway. "So do you. Although I think you probably meant it in an entirely differently way."

She recoiled as far as she could, hiding her thoughts from me, but her eyes were on my neck and her fingers twisted in my shirt as she breathed in through her mouth.

"Go ahead," I told her gruffly.

Her eyes flew to mine. "What?"

"If you want to feed," I said. "I'm offering."

She flashed her fangs on a hiss, and every hair on my body stood on end. My heart began to beat hard and fast, and she focused on the side of my throat, on the pulse pounding with the rush of my blood. My cock swelled to a painful state.

"I want to feel your teeth in me," I whispered. "I want to feed you. Fuck, Kenya, it makes me hard just thinking about it." Taking her hand again, I pressed her palm against the front of my jeans. "Do you feel that?" I asked her. "Do you feel what you do to me?"

With a groan, she flattened her back against the tomb behind her, drawing as far back as she could even as she squeezed the bulge in my pants. "I can't, Alex."

"Yes, you can," I insisted. "It's okay. I want you to." And because I thought if I could get her to drink from me, she wouldn't share that intimacy with anyone else. It was a fucked up reason, but I didn't care. I wanted to be everything for her. It was more than attraction. More than the fact that I liked it. So much more.

Gods, I was about to come just thinking about it.

But she shook her head and pulled her hand away from my cock. "No. No, I can't."

Bracing my hands on either side of her head, I leaned down, touching my forehead to hers, unable to keep myself from touching her. "Why not?"

There was a long pause. "Because I don't think I'll be able to stop," she confessed. "Please, Alex."

She could've easily pushed me away from her. Hell, she could've sent me flying out of the cemetery. But instead, she was asking me to give her some space, and so that's what I did. "Okay." I back up a step, then two more just for good measure. I wanted to scream my frustration to the sky. I wanted to rail at her. Wanted to insist she admit she felt the same unexplainable yearning for me that I felt toward her.

Instead, I scrubbed my face with my hands. When I had myself as under control as I was going to get, I only said, "But stay with me a little longer." Because I could feel the darkness welling up within me, and I needed the distraction.

Chewing on her bottom lip, she shoved her hands into the pockets of her coat and looked up at the sky.

"We have hours until sunrise," I told her.

"I can't stay that long."

"Okay."

She exhaled loudly. I could see in her eyes that she was torn, and it gave me hope. "Okay," she told me.

And so we talked. We talked about everything except the reason we were sneaking around to find time together. I learned we shared some favorite books, and what she did when wasn't at The Purple Fang. I told her everything I could about my life and being a warlock.

And while we talked, I got the chance to hold her hand, to play with her fingers, to touch her face, her throat, to listen to her soft voice and enjoy the sound of her laughter. I got to see her as she finally relaxed around me. I got to see her as herself.

And she was more than I ever imagined.

"I need to go, Alex," she finally said.

"I don't want you to." And I really didn't. I enjoyed her company more than I thought possible.

"I have to."

"I'll walk you home."

She shook her head. "No. You can't."

I clenched my jaw. "I don't like you roaming The Quarter alone."

"I'll run," she said with a smile. "Vamp speed."

Although she was smiling, I could tell there would be no arguing with her, so I gave in. "Let me know when you're in the house."

"Deal," she told me.

I walked her to the wall where she'd come in. She stopped and listened for a moment, then graced me with one last smile before she backed up a few steps and leapt the wall, landing silently on the other side.

By the time I let myself out of the gate, magically locking it behind me, she was gone. I'd only made it to the end of the block when I received a text.

Home. Thank you for tonight.

Then a few seconds later,

We can't do that again.

I laughed. Little things like agreements between covens and a scary djinn were not enough to keep me away from this female.

14

KENYA

I waited until Alex had left the graveyard before I hit send on my phone, alerting him to the fact that I was home safe and sound and not following him down the empty streets of New Orleans.

I was taking a huge risk. I knew this. But I had to know if I could trust him or if he was just feeding me a bunch of bullshit.

Djinn were known to be liars. Manipulative. Power hungry. It truly frightened me that this was in his blood. And if what he'd said was true, if it was activated the night he'd saved me, then perhaps he really wasn't the same guy he'd always been. Not that I'd known him well before, but I'd always had the impression he was a well-respected member of the Moss coven.

Besides, if anyone was a wild card there, it was the witch with the bright red hair and rebellious pale green eyes. I'd put money on that one any day.

But I couldn't help but worry that this was nothing but a game for him. What if he was lying about his power? What if Alex had been in cahoots with his djinn uncle all this time?

And did the entire witch coven know? Were they all just playing with us? What if the curse that almost killed me had been planned all along? Same as Alex being the one to save me? It would explain why I, the only female vampire and completely insignificant as far as coven hierarchy, was the one who was attacked.

Perhaps I was saved only so he could earn my trust. So he could seduce me and have an "in" into my coven. Get close to me, and therefore close to Killian.

I was an easy target for a male such as Alex.

My stomach dropped at the thought. But why else would Alex, who just a few weeks ago was insisting I didn't go anywhere alone or even stay at the club after closing time by myself, suddenly deem it perfectly safe for me to ditch that guard and have a secret meetup with him so we could make out in a graveyard? He'd told me I didn't need to worry about the djinn tonight. How would he know that? And why go from super cautious to completely blasé about the whole thing seemingly overnight?

Yeah, I wasn't stupid.

Even if he hadn't been in on the djinn's plans all along, maybe something had happened. He'd turned Alex somehow. Used our attraction to each other against him. Manipulated him.

Maybe the djinn was playing a game with the both of us.

I ground my teeth together as rage flooded through me. How dare he play with me this way.

And at that very moment, I couldn't have said which "he" I was talking about exactly, or which one I was angrier with, but I was done being at the center of their game. Done being the victim.

He didn't go to his car as I expected. Instead, I followed Alex as he walked past the high-rises all the way through the Warehouse District and under the expressway. Past the homeless humans living in tents. Hanging back, I watched with a mixture of feelings as Alex stopped and said hello, handing out cash like it was Monopoly money, even staying a few minutes to chat with one elderly man before continuing on his way.

Waiting until he got a couple of blocks ahead, I followed him, running past the humans too fast for them to see me.

At the corner of Jackson Ave and Saint Charles Ave I stopped, unable to follow him any further as he continued down the street. Magic pulsed in the air around The Garden District neighborhood like a forcefield, sure to alert the witches if I dared to cross the boundary. But that was okay because I'd found out what I'd needed to know. Alex was just going home.

With a sigh of relief, I turned down Saint Charles, following the tracks that ran down the center of the street all the way to Lee Circle. There, after making a face at the statue of Robert E. Lee, I took a seat on the steps of the monument and pulled out my phone. By some miracle, no one had tried to find me yet. Perhaps they assumed I'd come home with Brogan and was now tucked safely away in my bedroom for the day with a book. Brogan assuming I'd called Jamal, of course, and gotten home way before him.

Relieved, I set my cell phone on the step beside me. I needed some time to think away from the curious minds of my coven, where I didn't have to constantly monitor my thoughts for fear someone would accidentally—or purposely—pull something out of my head I wasn't ready for them to know.

I just needed a minute to figure out what I was feeling so I could shove those emotions way down before I was around the guys again. Because right now, I felt like a hundred different emotions were buzzing around inside of me, and the only commonality between them was that they all had something to do with a certain warlock named Alex Moss.

With a frown, I pushed that thought away. Though I really wanted to know, how he chose to identify himself wasn't important. Leaning back on my elbows, I watched a lonely pedestrian walk quickly down the sidewalk as I thought back to all of my interactions with Alex since he'd healed me. My mind quickly going over everything he'd said, the way he'd looked at me, the way he'd touched me.

His kisses.

His reaction when I'd kissed him back.

I squeezed my thighs together as I remembered it all in great detail. Surely, he couldn't have been faking that. I tasted nothing false in his kisses, felt nothing deceptive in his touch.

Or perhaps he was just a really good actor.

I pursed my lips, thinking about that. No. No, he couldn't be that good. And much as everyone liked to think otherwise, I wasn't that naive. There was honesty in the attraction between us. I'd felt it filling my hand tonight, for the sake of the gods. Saw it in his eyes and the way his entire body trembled in his effort to keep his need for me under control. Surely, he couldn't fake that. I knew I could trust that much at least.

Attraction, a funny word that didn't come close to describing the unceasing desperation I felt to be near him. All the time. Every moment. Even now, it was like there was an invisible thread connecting us even though we were far apart, pulling me in his direction. Like, somehow, when he'd reached inside of me to remove the curse, he'd left something of himself behind. And now he was a part of me.

And the way he played my body…gods. My heart began to race just thinking about it. I yearned to feel him against me, skin to skin. Dreamed of the taste of his blood. The way he moaned in my ear.

Or even just the way he watched me from across the room.

And he was always watching me.

Taking off my glasses, I closed my eyes and rubbed the bridge of my nose with my fingertips as I tried to tune out the physical reaction Alex invoked in me, set my emotions aside, and think about what was happening with us in a logical manner.

But it was impossible to separate the two. My physical need for Alex was inexplicably woven into my perception of him and what he told me to be true. It colored everything he said. Everything he did. And the way I reacted to it.

If I were to be truly logical about it though, I knew that we couldn't keep on the way we'd been. Sneaking around like teenagers. It was ridiculous. But what were my other choices?

Simple, I told myself. There was only one. To stop seeing him. My heart plummeted to my stomach, but I knew I was right. I wouldn't...no, I *couldn't* risk my family because my lady parts had the hots for a warlock.

Vivid memories of my human life assaulted me. Always poor. Always alone. None of the families who took me in ever formed any sort of attachment to me, nor I to them, really. I was never good enough to be someone's daughter. Or someone's sister. Though I desperately longed to be both of those. And I changed schools every time I switched foster parents, so I never had any chance to make friends. I was the shy kid with the ugly glasses who always had my nose stuck in a library book. Sometimes the kids were nice enough, other times they weren't. But most of the time they just ignored me. And on the rare occasion one of my classmates reached out to me, I would have to move before we could truly become friends. So, books became my constant companion. The characters in them the only friends I needed.

But the night I woke up as a vampire, all of that changed. Killian became my father, my friend, and my teacher. And what was more, he accepted me and cared about me even with all of my imperfections I carried over with me into my immortal life. The other guys took me under their wing, too. And before I knew it, I had an instant family who truly cared about each other and looked out for one another. Something I'd never known before.

They were the only ones who'd ever stuck their necks out for me. And I wasn't going to blow that all away now.

So tonight, I was going to go home and tell them all what was going on, and this time I wasn't leaving Alex out of the picture. Surely, once Killian and the others heard everything he'd done to keep me—and them—safe, they wouldn't be able to do anything but thank him. And Jamal could back up my story.

Mind made up, I was anxious to get home and stood up to leave. Before I could, however, I felt it. The dark magic that had been hunting me the other night. It slithered along my skin, worming its way beneath my clothes and leaving shivers in its wake.

The djinn was here.

I froze, my heart pounding in my chest. I needed to get the hell out of there, and I needed to do it now.

A man with dark hair and eyes appeared at the bottom of the monument, directly below me. Like a vampire, one second I was alone and the next he was there. He wore nothing but a dark long-sleeved sweater and dress slacks. Black shoes. Not what I was expecting to see on such an infamous supernatural creature. He looked...normal, harmless, except for the waves of ominous sorcery hitting me.

"Hello, vampire," he said in a pleasant voice. "It seems we meet again."

I ran. Spinning around, I took off up the steps to the statue and down the other side of the monument. My mind numb with fear, I didn't go in the direction of Killian and the others, but back down Saint Charles Ave.

It was Alex I ran to.

I hadn't gone a block when I felt something sink its claws into my hips and shoulders and I was lifted off the ground and sucked back the way I had come. A scream rose in my throat as my fangs shot down and the vampire in me instinctively readied itself for a fight, my muscles tensing and my mind going over every possible outcome within the span of a second.

But it was all for naught as I slammed into the front of the djinn and his arms wrapped around me like steel bands. Hissing and growling, I struggled like a banshee in his grip, but he only chuckled, holding me to his chest with little effort.

"Sleep," he whispered in my ear.

And then there was only blackness.

15

ALEX

"Where the fuck is she?"

It was Sunday, and Lizzy had closed the store and called an emergency meeting of the coven at her touristy voodoo shop—Ancient Magicks. We were all here: Judy, Alice, Talin, Angel, me, and Lizzy, of course.

It was also the middle of the day, so the last thing I'd expected was to have a pissed off vampire all up in my face. "Where is who?" I asked Jamal.

Lizzy put a hand on his arm. "Jamal," she admonished.

But he shook her off. "He knows where she is. Hell, he's probably the one who took her."

My blood froze as the implications of what he was telling me started to penetrate my thick skull. "What the fuck are you talking about?" I growled at him.

I swear, I wasn't a praying sort of guy. But at this moment, I would gladly fall to my knees and offer myself to any god who was listening just to have what I knew he was about to tell me not be true.

The conversation between me and Jamal had caught everyone's attention. "Kenya is missing," Lizzy told us. "I called this meeting to see if we could do some sort of a spell to find her. A tracking spell maybe?" She looked to Judy for confirmation.

The High Priestess was already hightailing it to the storage room, Talin and Alice on her heels. "How long has she been gone?" she called over her shoulder. "And does anyone have anything of Kenya's?"

"Wait." I held up my hands. "Her cell phone," I said to Lizzy and Jamal. "Can you track it somehow?"

"I did that last night when she never came home," Jamal told me. "I found it on the steps of the monument in Lee Circle."

Lee Circle? Halfway between my house and hers. What the fuck was she doing there? I shook my head. "No. That can't be right. She texted me and told me she was home."

Jamal nodded his head slowly, his mouth pulled tight and his eyes knowing. "So you *were* with her last night."

I found my phone and pulled up my text messages. "Look," I told them, turning the screen around so they could see it. "Right here. See?"

"Looks like she was lying to you," Jamal said with a smirk.

"How are you even fucking here?" I asked him, what little patience I had rapidly wearing thin. "Shouldn't you be dead to the world in your coffin right now?"

He just bared his teeth at me in something that in no way resembled a smile.

Lizzy put her hand on his arm again, but her attention was on me. "When did you last see her?" she asked me. When I didn't answer right away, she added in a quiet, "Jamal filled me in this morning."

I ran my hands through my hair. "So Killian knows." Weird that he would send Jamal instead of coming to kill me himself.

"No, he doesn't know about your part in all of this," she told me. "Jamal and I agreed that we should have the whole story before we told him anything."

"So he knows he has good reason to kill me without feeling guilty about it?" I was only half kidding.

"No one is killing anyone," Judy piped in from just behind the curtain. "We're ready to do the spell. Do you have something of Kenya's?" she asked Jamal.

"Yeah," he told her and handed over a piece of jewelry he'd had in his jeans pocket. A necklace. "I wasn't sure what to bring," he said. "She doesn't wear this all the time, but she wears it enough that I thought it would work." His expression was tight with worry as he waited for Judy's approval. "If not, Lizzy can maybe run back and grab a shirt out of her laundry or something."

"This will work fine," she told him, taking the necklace.

I saw Jamal's eyes flick past Judy and stay there. I looked over my shoulder to see who or what had stolen his attention, only to find Angel standing in front of the curtain that separated the two rooms, looking like she'd just stepped off the pages of a magazine with her white skin, green eyes, bright red hair, and matching lips. Not to mention the beaded designer sweater, perfectly fitted pants, and heeled boots that probably cost more than my rent. "Are we doing this?" she asked our aunt.

"Lizzy, we're going to need your help," Judy told her.

"But I don't know what I'm doing," she protested. "What if I mess it up?"

But my aunt just grabbed her hand and pulled her along behind her. "Doesn't matter," Judy said. "Alex. You, too."

I followed them into the storage room and back to the secret door that was normally hidden behind a rack of metal shelves, my mind racing and Jamal on my heels. I saw him breathe a sigh of relief as we entered the windowless room and had to give him props for being ballsy enough to show up here in Lizzy's shop with no one but her to protect him from being tossed out into the sun. Not that Judy would do that for no reason, but from my experience, vampires were distrustful creatures.

Without being told, my coven sisters and I formed a circle around the map spread out on the dirt floor, careful not to knock over the candles, and linked hands. Judy placed the necklace in the center of the circle and pulled Lizzy in between her and Talin. Jamal stood near the closed door, out of the way, one hand in his front pocket and the other rubbing the back of his neck in a nervous gesture.

I wanted to scream. I wanted to run out of the room and search every inch of the city until I found her, on foot if I had to. I couldn't stop thinking—what if she'd gotten caught in the sun?

Or worse, what if Marcus had changed his mind about her.

"Alex," Judy said, holding out her hand.

I looked over at her. Without a word, I put my hand in hers, noticing how it shook. Holding our arms out until our joined hands were over the map, she nicked my finger with a small knife, dripping a few drops of blood on the location of the Lee Monument on the map. I received a few looks from the others, but no one questioned Judy's decision to use my blood. If they didn't know about my connection to before, they sure as hell did now.

Judy handed me a bandage from her pocket, and I wrapped up my finger then took my place in the circle.

Hands linked and eyes closed, we began to chant the locator spell as one, repeating it over and over as we gave our magic over to the spell, feeding it into the blood on the map. The air moved around us, stirring my hair and my clothes, and goose bumps rose up all over my skin. When I felt the blood begin to move, I opened my eyes and saw the others do the same. We continued chanting the spell, watching it move west across the map out of the city.

As it entered the swampland, it slowed down. I exchanged glances with Alice and as one, the coven began to chant louder, our voices strong and insistent. The drop of blood shuttered, moved a fraction of an inch, and exploded, splattering all over the map.

It was finished.

I stared at the blood covered paper. No. *No*. She couldn't be lost to me.

Jamal took a few steps toward us, his eyes shifting nervously around the room. "What happened? Where is she? Did you see?"

"The spell was blocked," Judy told him.

"What does that mean?" he asked her.

"It means it's finished. There's nothing more we can do here," I told him as I stared down at the map.

Jamal stomped forward as we all unlinked our hands, breaking the circle. He looked down at the map, then at me, then at Judy. "There's got to be something else. What if we brought you something else? I can find you some of her hair or something."

"Jamal, it's the middle of the day," Lizzy reminded him.

"Okay," he said. "Then you can run home and find it."

But Judy just shook her head. "It won't do any good, Jamal. The spell is blocked. There's nothing we can do."

His head whipped around. Wide eyes locking on each of us in turn. "What the fuck is that supposed to mean? You're witches. You have to find her."

"So, we're done?" Angel left the circle and started to leave.

As I stood, frozen and numb, Jamal flew across the room, blocking the door. "Where the fuck do you think you're going?" he asked her in a low voice.

She took a step back and turned her head away. I noticed she wouldn't meet my eyes, or anyone's. "Tell him to let me pass," she said in Lizzy's direction.

"You're not going anywhere, Leeloo," he told her.

Angel finally looked up at him. "What did you call me?"

He moved his head forward, jutting out his chin and putting his mouth right in her face. "*Leeloo*," he told her.

She gave him the same attitude right back. "And *why* are you calling me that?" she asked.

"Because you have hair like Leeloo in *The Fifth Element*."

Angel crossed her arms over her chest and laughed. "No, I don't."

"Yeah, you do."

"Her hair is orange. Mine is cherry red."

"Still looks like hers," he argued. "And you're still not fucking leaving, *Leeloo*, until I know where Kenya is."

"ENOUGH," I told them.

Angel threw her arms up in the air and stomped away. Judy gave me a warning glare, but I ignored it. "I'll find her," I told them all. I felt cold. Numb. But my mind was racing and my heart was pounding in my chest.

"How are you gonna do that, witch?" Jamal asked when I walked up to him.

My upper lip lifted in a sneer. "You're just going to have to trust me," I told him.

"I don't trust anything about you," he replied.

We stared each other down for a few minutes, but whatever he saw in my eyes must have been enough, for he stepped away from the door. "You know what? You do that. You find her. And you'd better do it before Killian can leave the house."

He didn't need to tell me why he was giving me that particular warning. The master vampire was probably losing his shit. I went to walk by but he grabbed my arm.

"Wait. Give me your phone."

"I don't have time for this shit, vampire."

"Give. Me. Your. Fucking. Phone."

I thought about blasting him out of my way, but then I saw the panic in his eyes. Pulling it from my pocket, I swiped the screen and entered my passcode, then handed it to him.

"Here's my number," he told me. "You call me the minute you find her. Understand?"

"Yeah," I told him.

"The fucking minute," he insisted, then shoved my phone into my chest. "And know the only reason I'm letting you go is because I'm fucking stuck here until the sun goes down. So you'd better not let me down, witch."

I took it from him and slid it back into the pocket of my coat. "I got it," I gritted through my teeth.

He held me there a minute, his jaw tight and his eyes anxious, then he let me go and walked away.

Looking back at Judy, I gave her a nod and walked out of the room.

I knew who'd taken Kenya.

Now, I just had to let him find me.

16

ALEX

I rushed out of Ancient Magicks only to stop just outside the store. Standing in the middle of the sidewalk, I looked up and down the street, completely clueless as to which way to go despite my assurance to the others. Tourists walked around me to peer into the shop's windows, looking at the displays before casting strange glances in my direction.

Where to go? Where to go?

The Garden District, maybe. It was where he'd found me before, and with all of the witches back at Lizzy's shop, it would be the safest place for us to have this conversation.

I started to walk toward Canal Street to catch the streetcar, but halfway there, I stopped again. I suddenly had the inexplicable feeling that this was all wrong. I didn't know how I knew that; I just did.

I needed to play this smart, not go rushing off half-cocked. I couldn't fuck this up, or Kenya could be lost to me forever. And the more time that went by, the more certain I became that Marcus was at the center of her disappearance, and that it had nothing to do with Kenya and everything to do with me. I had no idea what he planned to do with her, but I would do whatever the fuck he wanted if he just let her live.

As I walked down the sidewalk as quickly as I could without drawing undo attention, I'd never been more grateful she was a creature of the night. Wherever he had her, he couldn't risk moving her during the day if he wanted to keep her alive. And if by some chance he didn't have her, perhaps the best place to begin searching was the last place I'd seen her.

I turned up Conti Street. I hadn't walked two blocks when I could feel the djinn's presence. I stumbled over a break in the sidewalk, my chest tight with fear. Not for me, but for Kenya. Although I'd believed this entire time Marcus was behind her disappearance, a part of me had hoped it wasn't true. That she had just gone somewhere and lost track of the time—maybe to feed—and forgotten her phone. And she was just hiding out somewhere waiting for the sun to go down.

The breeze picked up, changing direction, and with it I was able to pinpoint the direction I needed to go. He was close, but not close enough.

I started walking faster. Past the Prince Conti Hotel with its flying flags and wrought iron details. Past the Three Legged Dog tavern, and across Rampart Street. At the church on the corner, I stopped again, closing my eyes and opening myself to the call of the djinn.

His magic felt different than what I was used to, yet also so very familiar. It was easy for me to follow. Or maybe he was laying out a trail of breadcrumbs, waiting for me to walk blindly into his trap. Either way, it didn't matter. I might be playing his game, but I'd be walking into it with my eyes wide open.

I was almost there.

A few minutes later, I found myself standing outside of the cemetery where I'd met Kenya the night before. He was here. I felt it all the way to my bones. And how fucking poetic. I guess this was his way of telling me that I'd been fucking stupid last night, thinking just because I couldn't sense him around, we were safe to be together. His way of telling me that I, because of my raging need to see her, was the one who'd put her right into his path.

My teeth began to ache and I realized I was clenching my jaw. Forcing myself to relax somewhat I stopped by the gate, blending in with the group of people about to take a tour, easily convincing the tour guide I'd been there the entire time with a few softly spoken words. Once inside, I lost the group and slipped around a tomb, then headed toward the djinn.

I found Marcus at the back, leaning casually against a tall statue. He smiled when he saw me. "Hello, nephew."

I stopped a safe distance away. "Where is she, Marcus?"

He cocked his head to the side. "Don't you think you should start calling me 'Uncle Marcus'?"

"No," I told him. "Now tell me where she is, and what you're planning to make me do to get her back so I can tell you to fuck off and go get her."

His smile faltered a bit. "You remind me of my brother. I didn't like him much."

I didn't respond, and eventually, he gave an exaggerated sigh.

"Fine. We'll get right to business."

"That would be fuckin' nice."

His expression tightened. It was so brief I might have missed it if I hadn't been paying attention. "I can tell you're eager to know about your lady love, so I will tell you now, the vampire is fine," he said.

"I want her back." This last was practically spit at him.

"I'm afraid that's not possible." He pushed himself away from the tomb and came to stand in front of me. "I need her."

My heart stopped, only to start up again, hard and fast. I tried to calm myself down, knowing he would sense my fear. "You don't need her." If this was his way of trying to win me over, I had some bad news for him.

"Oh, but I do. And contrary to what you're thinking right now, it really has very little to do with you."

Nothing to do with me? Why the hell else would he want her? Memories of her lying in bed, rotting from the inside out as she died before my eyes, flashed through my mind. Terror for Kenya had me unable to speak for a long moment. And when I could, all I could do was grind out through my teeth, "What are you talking about?"

But he just smiled. "I'll tell you what you want to know. But first, let's talk terms, shall we?"

Linking his hands behind his back, he started to pace back and forth in front of me. I took the opportunity to reach into my pocket and wrap my fingers around my cell phone as I tried to think of a way to alert the others without pulling it out of my pocket. If I could manage to get the screen open and call someone by feel, maybe he wouldn't hear it ring or the person who answered, what with all of the cars driving by and the chatter from the people touring the place.

My only other option was to try to reach out to Alice through our bond. I've never done it before, but that didn't mean it wouldn't work. We weren't only witches, we were twins. Twins did that all the time, right?

Marcus suddenly stopped his pacing. His head snapped up and his dark eyes zeroed in on me. "I wouldn't, if I were you."

My hand froze on my phone. I had no idea if I'd managed to type in my code by feel or not, or to get the damn thing to call anyone. "Wouldn't what?"

"Please, Alex. I'm not stupid, nor am I gullible. So let's stop pretending that I am." He walked closer to me until he was only an arm's length away. "Let's get one thing out in the open right now, shall we?"

After a pause, I nodded once.

"If you try to contact your sister or any of your coven through magic or more modern means," he cast a meaningful glance down at my coat pocket where my hand was still wrapped around my phone, "I will know. Doing any of those things will force me to take more drastic measures to get what I want, and I don't think either of us would want anything to *happen* to Alice or any of the others."

"You wouldn't hurt Alice." I called his bluff. "She's your niece."

"Yes, she is. But I have found in my observations of her that she's not nearly the djinn you are."

His tone told me exactly what he thought of anyone, family or not, who didn't carry enough of his genes. They were disposable, just like any other human. "She's a powerful witch," I said, remembering what he'd told me the first time we'd talked. If he thought she was worthy of keeping alive, perhaps it would remove her from the equation.

"Her powers are limited to simple tricks of nature. Nothing that any witch worth his or her salt couldn't do."

He was wrong. Alice was way more than a simple Wiccan. But I quickly forced all thoughts of her from my mind, not wanting him to leach them from my head.

Marcus lowered his chin, his eyes never leaving my face. "Have I made myself absolutely clear?"

"Yeah. Perfectly."

"Excellent." He grinned at me and resumed his pacing. "So, here are my terms."

I pulled my hand from my pocket, crossed my arms over my chest, and waited for him to lay it all out. As he began to talk, my mind raced, thinking of and discarding any and every way I could think of to get Kenya and I out of this mess. But he'd been smart to meet me here, in public, with tourists all around. He knew I wouldn't do anything to put them in harm's way or to blow our cover.

In the end, with him always one step ahead, there was nothing I could do. At least, for now. I'd just have to bide my time and wait for the right opportunity.

"As I told you the other day, Alex, I want you to come live with me. I want us to spend time together. Get to know each other. We are family, after all. And no matter how much you try to deny it to yourself, or to others, we are much more alike than you think."

"You're wrong," I told him. "I'm nothing like you."

He showed no reaction to my argument. In fact, he fucking ignored me completely, continuing his speech as though I hadn't spoken.

"There are advantages to coming to live with me. Some you might have already thought of. Or perhaps not." He stopped directly in front of me, raking his eyes from my head to my waterproof boots and back again. "You're strong, Alex. Your magic is powerful. But it's not nearly as powerful as it could be if you learned to harness it. To twist it to your will. Tell me, do the spirits talk to you?"

"What?" The dude was crazy. Of course, if he spent his days hearing voices, that kind of explained a lot. "No. No, I don't fucking hear voices. I'm not crazy."

"Hmm," he nodded his head. "You've blocked them. Probably figured out how to do it as a child, which not very many djinn can do." He waved his hand through the air. "That's all right. We can open you back up to them."

My entire body was beginning to ache from the constant tension stiffening my muscles all of this time. I had no patience for this shit. But other than attacking him in front of all of these people, people who were even now making their way closer and closer to us as the tour progressed through the cemetery, I had no choice but to stand here and listen to him ramble on about shit that made absolutely no sense, and hope that he'd eventually take me to Kenya.

Besides, I didn't know that I would win. If I went after him he might just leave, or kill me, and then I'd never find out where she was.

So I stood there like a well-behaved student, listening to him go on and on about spirits and magic and other dimensions and how he could "help" me learn about all of this fucking power I had no intention of tapping into if it meant I would turn into a creature like him. I played along, even though my blood was rushing through my body until I felt lightheaded and there was a constant buzzing in my head obstructing his words.

I stood there, half-listening, letting him talk himself out. The only thing on my mind getting to Kenya and trying to figure out how I could get us both the hell away from him and off of his radar.

Because I wasn't stupid, either. And I knew there was no way I could take him out if he saw it coming.

However, as his words flowed over me, there was a part of me—a very small part—that was paying attention to everything he was saying. This part of me wondered what it would be like to be as all-powerful as the djinn. To have everyone afraid of me. To not have to live by rules put in place by others. To be able to live how I wanted. To love who I wanted. With no fear of repercussions. This part of me was not afraid. This part of me was open to the seduction.

And it scared me more than the djinn.

"If you agree to my terms," Marcus went on. "I will take you to the vampire. And you can have her once I'm done with her. IF, and only if, you stay with me. Learn from me. Become my true family. Then, and only then, will I give you my blessing to be with the vampire."

"Kenya," I told him. "Her name is Kenya."

He smiled. "I am well aware of her name."

"Then why don't you use it?" I had no idea why I was picking a fight over something so asinine. But I couldn't seem to stop myself. It was like I needed to have a win here. Just one win. So I didn't feel so completely powerless.

"Because she means nothing to me," he said. "She is a means to an end. An object. I need her to help me get my love back, and that's all. Once she's done that, you can have her, and she can be 'Kenya' to you."

Get his love back? Wait, what the hell did I miss?

"Do you agree to come with me? To learn how to be a djinn? To be a family?" He appeared right in front of me, nose to nose, and I didn't even see him move. Dark sorcery wrapped around me, squeezing me like a constrictor until I couldn't breathe.

"And you must mean it, my nephew. Don't think you can pull the wool over my eyes because I will know. I know everything about you. Everything you think. Everything you feel. And though I understand you may have some natural hesitations, that is all it must be." He backed up a step, and I sucked in a breath as he released me.

"Now," he said. "Do we have an agreement?"

What fucking choice did I have? "Yes." The word tasted like metal on my tongue. "If you take me to Kenya right fucking now."

Marcus smiled, and this time it was true. "Then let's go see your vampire."

17

KENYA

I sat in the corner of the kitchen of the swamp house with my knees pulled up to my chest and my arms wrapped around my legs—the same house where Killian had hidden me when I was ill—and watched the sun as it crept toward me along the floor. There would come a point where I would have to either risk it and move, fast enough that I won't catch on fire as I cross the floor, or just let it burn me alive.

I wasn't sure yet which option I was going to take.

I'd woken up from the djinn's sleep on the couch, blinking against the sunshine coming in through the window of the living room. Sunshine I hadn't seen in eighty years. Another five minutes, maybe less, and it would've been on me. With a hiss, I'd scrambled off of the couch and ran toward the back of the house, where Killian and Jamal had sealed the windows so we would be safe to spend our days here. I'd completely forgotten that most of it had been demolished by Killian's anguish when he'd come here after Lizzy had left him. She'd come back, but the house had never been fixed. And now there were giant holes in the walls and roof.

Veering to the right, I'd gone into the kitchen, frantically opening cabinets as I looked for a place to hide for the day. But they were all too small for me to fit into, and none of the doors fit right, leaving cracks where the light could get through even if I'd managed to get into them somehow. This house had once been a place for crocodile hunters to find shelter. It wasn't meant to be a home, and therefore only had the minimum requirements to keep a human semi-comfortable for a short period of time.

Faced with the option of either burning slowly or just getting it over with in one fell swoop, I'd curled up in the corner, far from the large window over the sink and the threat of day. Yet, in my panicked state, I'd forgotten what time of year it was and how I'd just lined myself up perfectly to be held captive by the encroaching sunset. Because once it started to go down, it would come right through the kitchen window, eventually brightening the entire room before it sank below the horizon.

And, in the time it had taken me to find this spot, the sun had already moved to the side of the house. I could probably get around it if I ran fast enough, but I didn't know what I'd be running into when I got to the other room. Disoriented by the time of day and the brightness, I couldn't seem to think straight.

I didn't know how much time had passed when the front door opened and two sets of footsteps trod across the wooden floor of the living room.

"Where the fuck is she?"

Alex?

It sounded like him, and yet...it didn't.

One set of footsteps approached the kitchen entry. I held completely still and waited, afraid to hope.

But it wasn't my warlock who appeared to rescue me, but the djinn. "What are you doing?" he asked. "Do you *want* to roast yourself?"

I'd kind of been thinking about it, yeah.

With a look of disgust, he waved his hand, and I watched as the blinds lowered and heavy curtains I hadn't even noticed before pulled themselves closed, blocking out the rays of the sun, except for two thin strips of light on the walls on either side. After sitting there so long, I blinked in the sudden darkness as someone else came to stand beside the djinn.

I recognized him right away, even before my vision cleared enough to make out the blurry details of his face.

"Where are her glasses?" he asked the djinn.

When all he got was a shrug, he left the room and his boots trod back across the wooden floor.

I got to my feet slowly, wondering what was going on. Why was he here with the djinn? Did he come alone? And why weren't they fighting?

I had a sinking feeling he wasn't here to help me, and that I'd been right all along.

At that moment, he came back into the kitchen and tried to hand me something. I could only stand there, staring at his blurry face, hoping against hope I was wrong and looking for some sign this was all some sort of a trick.

"Kenya," he said, holding his hand up higher. "Here's your glasses."

His voice was cold. Hard. I felt as though I were outside my body, watching as my hand slowly reached out and took them from him. My eyes never left his face as I opened them up and put them on.

Alex studied me, a look in his golden eyes I couldn't read. Behind him, the djinn was watching us with interest. "As you can see," he said. "The vampire is alive and well."

I frowned as Alex, with one last sweeping look at me, turned away. "She wouldn't have been if we hadn't gotten here when we had. I thought she was so important to you."

The djinn looked over at me. "I left her on the couch. She was perfectly safe."

I was so confused. Why was he talking about me like I was some sort of animal without a mind of my own, and why was Alex acting the same way?

"When do we leave?" he asked the djinn.

"Tomorrow night. I have something I must do before we go."

"What are you talking about?" I asked him. "Go where?"

The djinn—what was his name? Marcus?—leveled a stare at me. Then he sighed. "I suppose it wouldn't hurt to fill you in. The sooner you know, the sooner I can have what I want."

I glanced over at Alex, but he wouldn't look at me. I had to admit, it hurt worse than I thought it would, his betrayal. Even though I kinda knew it was coming. My instincts had told me all along that he couldn't be trusted. And as usual, they were right. He'd been in on this all along.

But if that were the case, then what I didn't understand was why hadn't he just taken me to the djinn himself? It would've been so easy. Last night, he could've handed me over to him with little fuss. I never would've suspected a thing because I, in my infatuation with him, had trusted him completely when he'd told me it was safe. When he'd told me that he was as taken with me as I was with him.

I'd been stupid. And naive. And...stupid.

"Vampire? Are you even listening?"

I blinked rapidly, clearing my head and turning my attention back to the djinn. "What?"

He exhaled loudly through his nose. "If you're not going to pay attention, I'm not going to waste my time standing here talking to you."

"I'm sorry," I murmured. Then could've kicked myself. What the hell was I apologizing for? This thing had kidnapped me!

But he seemed to take some measure of pity on me, for his expression softened a bit. "You won't be harmed," he told me. "As long as you do what I need you to do."

"And what is it you think you need from me?" I asked him. I was still standing in the corner of the kitchen, afraid to move. The djinn were nothing I ever wanted to mess with. And even if I could somehow sneak up on him and tear his head off, at this point in time I had no idea how Alex would react.

"I need you to bring someone back from the dead."

I glanced at Alex, but he was staring at the floor and no help at all. "Like, make someone a vampire?" Did he want to create vampires? Why?

"No, not a vampire. A witch. She died about forty years ago."

Confused, I looked between him and Alex. "You kidnapped me because you think I'm some sort of necromancer?"

"Not think. I know."

I shook my head, holding my hands in front of me in supplication. "Look. I don't know what you think you know, but you've got it all wrong. I'm nothing but a nerdy girl who was made into a less than extraordinary vampire that my maker decided to keep around anyway. Maybe to keep him and the rest of the guys from becoming complete Neanderthals, I don't know, but anyway, he did. I don't know anything about magic, or raising the dead, or...or...anything like that."

He tilted his head. "How little you know of yourself."

I dropped my arms back down to my sides. "What is that supposed to mean?"

With a smirk, he glanced at Alex. I was glad to see he didn't return it. Although it didn't change anything about what was going on here. When the djinn looked back at me, the smirk was still there. "It means there is more to you than your family ever told you. Your human family," he specified.

"I never knew my human family," I admitted. "I was given up for adoption right after I was born."

"And your adopted parents wouldn't know where you'd come from, I gather." Though he said the words aloud, I got the impression he was speaking more to himself than to me.

I answered anyway. "I was never adopted. I just got bounced around foster homes until I was old enough to live on my own."

"Really?" He seemed genuinely surprised. "Did you know this?" he asked Alex.

"I did," he said, finally glancing in my direction. But he looked away again just as quickly.

Affronted, the djinn asked, "Well, why didn't you tell me?"

A flash of anger tightened Alex's expression, but it was there and gone before I could guess what it meant. "Because you only just told me what you wanted her for on the way here. And because you didn't ask."

The djinn waved away his answer. "Technicalities."

"Look," I interrupted. "I can't help you. So there's no reason for you to keep me here." I honestly didn't know what was going on between him and Alex, but I had to worry about myself. And right now, my happy ass wanted nothing more than to get the hell out of there alive and in one piece. I was feeling more alert, and I could tell by the easing up of the prickles on my skin that the sun was setting.

Which meant I could get the hell out of there.

"Except you can't," the djinn answered my unspoken thoughts. "I've taken precautions against that very thing."

What precautions?

"Go ahead," he said. "Try to walk out the door if you need proof to believe me."

With the two males blocking the entry, and the djinn's sorcery coiling around me since the moment he walked into the room, I wasn't about to try to get past them. "I'll take your word for it." For now.

"Good. Then let's talk, shall we?" The djinn went over to the small table and took a seat, indicating that I should do the same.

Not seeing that I had any other choice, I walked over to the table and sat down.

"Thank you," he told me. "There's really no reason this needs to be hard on either of us. We can work together and get me what I want, and then you will be free of my service."

"And free to leave?" I asked. It was stupid to hope it would be that easy, I knew. Or even that he would be telling the truth. But still, I had to ask.

"You will be free of my service," he repeated.

Which meant I would never be able to come back here to my family. "Wait," I said as a horrible thought occurred to me. "By 'free of your service', does that mean I'll still be alive? Or do you just plan to 'free' me by lopping off my head?"

He seemed slightly surprised by my question. "I see no reason why we can't part ways amicably."

Not really a straight answer to my question, but I guess that's all I was getting for now. "Okay. I guess that'll have to be good enough for now. But, can I ask, why did you try to kill me before if you need me so much now?"

"That's simple," he told me. "That was an experiment that didn't work out quite the way I'd hoped. However, it all worked out in the end because it wasn't until after my nephew had healed you that I discovered who you truly are. And let me tell you, I'm so very happy I didn't kill you as planned."

He spoke of my death so casually. Like it was nothing at all. "Yeah, me too."

"As you have no knowledge of your ancestry, I would think you're dying to know."

Not really. Once I'd gotten old enough to realize what my so-called "mother" had done, I figured if they didn't care enough to try to stop her, I didn't care enough to know them. "Yes. Okay."

He put his elbow on the table and his chin on his hand. "I'm going to be blunt, because we don't have a lot of time, and I need you to be on board with this. You may actually be pleasantly surprised by what I'm about to tell you."

"And what is that?"

"That you are not only a vampire, but you're a vampire who has the blood of voodoo queens running through your veins."

I sat back in my chair. "No, I don't."

"Ah, but you do. And it's that blood, combined with your vampirism, that makes you able to do what I need you to do."

"Raise the dead," I said.

"Raise the dead," he confirmed.

18

JESSE

SEATTLE, WA

I looked around the living room of Luukas's apartment. The vampires were all there: Luukas, Nikulas, Aiden, Christian, Dante—nervously standing closest to the door—and of course, my Shea.

The witches were there, standing or seated near their vampire mates: Keira, Emma, Grace, Ryan, Laney…

And myself.

"The floor is yours, warlock," Luukas announced, then pulled Keira from his favorite chair and settled her on his lap.

I nodded my thanks. Ten sets of eyes settled on me, some nervous, others openly hostile. Shea squeezed my hand, then took a seat on the arm of the couch near where I stood.

"Before we go on to anything else, there's something you all need to know. And especially you, Ryan." I turned to my sister. She sat before the fireplace in the furthest corner of the room, Christian beside her. But with her bright hair reflecting the multitude of colors of the rising sun, porcelain skin, and sapphire blue eyes, it would be impossible for her to go unnoticed, even if she wore boring clothes. However, her preference seemed to be skirts or pants that matched her bright colored tops.

I blamed this horrendous sense of style on the fact that Christian had found her in Tijuana, stripping to support her drug habit. The habit she'd acquired to try to silence the voices in her head, the same voices that whispered to me. But she wasn't crazy as she once thought, she just had a natural connection to the world of spirits the others would never be able to achieve. It was our djinn blood that opened us to other world and dimensions.

I also knew that now, instead of using drugs, she was using Christian's blood as a way to silence the voices. They weren't silenced, however, only controlled. The vampire blood strengthened her own powers without any effort on her part.

Something we would have to remedy.

Her bright eyes were wide as she stared up at me, as she didn't like being the center of attention. At least not here, where she felt the other witches didn't like her. But it wasn't that they didn't approve of her, they just knew she was different, like myself, and that made them nervous.

Just wait until they saw how powerful she would become.

I walked over and sat down on my heels before her. Not too close. I didn't want to rile up her mate, fun as that would be. But we didn't have time for it right now. "There's something you need to know," I told her. "Something that's going to be hard for you to hear, and you probably won't believe me, but everything I'm about to tell you is absolutely true."

"And what is it you need to tell me?" she asked, surprising me. Though I probably shouldn't have been. My sister was stronger than a lot of people gave her credit for. The fact that she wasn't nervous around me like the others were was proof of that.

From the corner of my eye, I saw Christian lean toward her. Offering her his support? His protection? Probably both. I allowed him this much, wishing I could touch her, take her hand, but knowing he would never allow it. "There's no easy way to say this, so I'm just going to come right out with it."

Her blue eyes travelled over my face. "Okay."

"Ryan...you're my sister. My twin, as I just told Luukas earlier."

Her eyes flew to the master vampire seated behind me. I assume he confirmed my words somehow, for her attention then came back to me. "How is that possible?"

"We were separated shortly after birth. You were taken away from me and adopted by a family who believed they couldn't have children. Although, I think they did manage to have a child somewhere down the line."

She nodded. "Yes."

I studied her face, looking for a sign. "I wish there was more time to discuss this, but for right now, I just need to know: do you believe me?" I asked her.

After a long pause, she said, "I do."

Good. This was good. "You get your hair from our mother, by the way. Same as your eyes. She was beautiful, much like you. And she was a very strong witch. Until our father killed her." I paused, overcome with emotion I only now allowed myself to feel. "There's so much I want to share with you. So much I want to teach you—"

"I don't think there's anything she needs to learn from you," Christian growled.

Ryan laid her hand on his leg, and he reluctantly sheathed his fangs.

Though I spoke to him, my eyes never left my sister. "I can show her how to control the voices. How to work with them. How to bring out her true magic, her power—"

He interrupted me again. "So you can teach her to be like you? Absolutely fucking not."

I finally deigned to look at him. "I believe that should be up to Ryan, don't you? She is a fully grown witch, after all."

The muscles clenched in his jaw, but he kept his mouth shut.

When I looked back at Ryan, her blue eyes were shiny with tears. "Can you really show me how to control the voices?"

I gave her a nod. "I can. They're not so bad once you learn how to get them to work for you, and how to shut them out when you don't want to be bothered."

"I'd like that," she told me.

"Good," I said. "We'll talk more later."

"Not alone," Christian gritted out.

Placing my hands on my thighs, I rose to my full height, rubbing my palms on my black pants. "Of course," I agreed. "Until she gets tired of having you babysit her."

"Jesse," Shea warned me.

With a hint of a smile, I acknowledged her warning. "Whatever makes you more comfortable," I told him.

I understood where he was coming from, I did. I was equally protective of my Shea, although I knew full-well she could easily protect herself.

Joining my vampire, I ran my hand over her dark hair. I took an unhealthy amount of satisfaction in the fact that I was the only male able to touch her thus. If any other took such liberties she would be screaming in pain, the remnants of a curse we had yet to figure out how to lift. One that, for my own selfish reasons, I wasn't sure I wanted to remove.

She smiled at me, and my heart raced within my chest.

It was with great effort I tore my eyes from her stunning face to give my attention to the rest of the group. "As you all know, I gave up my army of demons—the army I was going to use to kill my father—for the love of this female and you, her family. In return, I was promised that you all would help me figure out a way to remove him from the throne of the Moss witch coven, where he currently reigns as the High Priest, and take his life."

"What makes you fucking think we're going to keep that promise?" Dante asked.

Before I could answer, Luukas spoke up. "We will keep it. I gave my word."

"To a fucking warlock who tortured you for seven years?" Dante shook his head, his dark eyes locked onto me. "I don't fucking think so."

"I gave my word," Luukas told him. "And I intend to keep it. If not for him, then for Shea."

At the mention of her name, Dante's dark eyes dropped to her where she sat on the arm of the couch beside me.

"Dante, please," she said. "This is not just for me or for Jesse, it's also for Laney and all of the other witches here whose families ran from their own coven in fear."

"Laney will stay here with me."

"Yes," Shea agreed. "But what of her family who are still there?"

"Why not just send him back to his own world?" Nikulas asked.

"Because he has the book that contains the spell to do that, and because even if we did, he keeps finding a way to come back," I told him. "His own brother took him back in 1947. Forty years later, he returned and killed his brother and the witch they both loved, taking over the coven. Then, years later, our mother"—I glanced over at Ryan—"sent him back again. With the help of a young witch he'd enthralled, he returned when I was a still a very young man, and he killed her." He paused. "He again took over the position of High Priest, sucking the magic from the coven until the witches were too weak to oppose him. Only the ones who'd managed to escape, like myself, were able to hang onto their magic. With a little help from my spirit friends and a witch or two who are still within the coven, I've been watching him, hoping for a chance to get my hands on that book, with no luck."

Linking my hands behind my back, I began to pace as I thought out loud. "So, I've decided to kill him. It's the only way to keep him from coming back."

Shea stood and grabbed my arm. "Jesse, you didn't tell me this."

I stopped, removing her hand from my arm and twining her fingers in mine. "I know. I'm sorry. I didn't want you to worry."

She stared up at me, her green eyes darkened with concern.

"Do you think you can do it?" Keira asked.

Glancing over at her, I said, "I am the only thing in this world that is a threat to him."

Luukas spoke up. "Then why has he allowed you to live?"

"That's the question I've been asking myself," I told him.

"Wait," Keira held up her hand. "If you can kill your father—a *djinn*—then why wait until now? Why did you need to create the demon army?"

"Because, until now, he's kept himself hidden away on the mountain of your ancestors, surrounded by witches whose magic he could reinstate at the slightest sign of a threat."

"But aren't you the great Oz, all mighty and powerful?" Aiden asked. He waved his hand in the air. "I can feel that power scurrying about the room from here."

"I am," I said. "But even sorcery such as mine could be hampered if fifty witches all attacked me at once. Long enough for my father to get away. The demons were to keep the witches busy, so I could get to my father with no resistance." Even I could hear the bitterness in my voice. I'd done the right thing, helping Shea send the demons back. And I don't know that she ever would've forgiven me if I hadn't. But still, it *irked* me.

"So, what's changed?" Luukas asked. "Other than the fact we have five very capable witches here to help you?"

"What's changed is that just last night I was informed my father is no longer hiding on his mountain but is alone and exposed. However, I have no idea how long he'll be this way."

"Which is where the sudden urgency comes from," Luukas surmised.

"That's correct."

The master vampire shared a look with his mate, then turned back to me. "What do you need us to do?"

"I need you to keep Shea here."

She pulled her hand from mine and stomped around to confront me, her lovely face animated in her anger. "Yeah, that's not happening, Jesse. And you damn well know it."

I smiled down at her and brushed a stray strand of hair away from her eyes. "I know. But it was worth a try." Pulling her against me, I whispered for her ears only, "I would die if anything happened to you, love."

"As would I," she responded. "Quite literally." Pulling away enough that she could look at me, she added, "But that's not the only reason I need to go with you to make sure you stay safe."

"I know."

Dropping a kiss on her dark hair, I looked up and met Luukas's eyes over the top of her head. "Originally, I wanted you to agree to allow everyone to come to the mountain with me. Between the vampires and the power of the witches here, I was hoping it would be enough to distract the others long enough for me to get to my father."

Shea pulled away to return to her seat, and with a bit of reluctance, I let her go.

"But, I don't understand," Emma said. "Why would the witches there fight for him? If we all showed up, children of the coven, wouldn't they help us?"

I shook my head. "No."

"Why not?" she asked.

"Yeah, I don't get it, either," Grace added.

"Because my father is a master of manipulation. He turned the loyalties of their parents by force and kept the loyalty of the children through fear. I'm sure by now he has them thoroughly convinced the world will end if they dare to worship another."

"And now that he is no longer on the mountain?" Dante asked.

"Now I would like you to come as backup. My father is in New Orleans. I'm not sure why he felt the need to travel there alone, but I'm sure the spirits will let me know as soon as they figure it out. What I do know is there is a coven of witches who reside in the Garden District, the High Priestess one who fled from the mountain when Marcus returned."

"More of us?" Keira asked.

I gave her a nod. "But there is also a coven of vampires. Apparently, they've come to some kind of agreement with the witches and live peacefully in The Quarter. I need you to help me make sure they don't interfere with what I need to do."

"That would be Killian Rice," Luukas said thoughtfully. "I'll call him and explain what's going on. I haven't talked to him in a long time, but I'm sure he'll allow us into his territory once I explain why we need to be there."

"Maybe he'll even have more info on Marcus," Keira added.

"If they even know he's there," I told them. "All I need is one opportunity to confront my father with no outside interference."

Luukas looked around the group before bringing his attention back to me, feeling out their reactions. They were reluctant to help me but would follow where their master told them to go. With a nod, he gave me his agreement.

"Looks like we're going to New Orleans." Nikulas grinned at Aiden and held up his hand for a high five.

I watched Luukas closely, gauging his reaction. I didn't know that he was ready for another battle just yet. "Perhaps you should stay here," I told him. "Although I would need Keira to come with me to talk to the High Priestess."

His arms tightened protectively around his witch. "Keira does not go anywhere I don't go."

"Guess it's settled then," Shea said from beside me.

Yes. Yes, it was.

Finally, after all these years, I was about to see my father again.

19

ALEX

As I stood there in the kitchen of the house where Kenya had nearly lost her life just a few weeks before, I couldn't help but have a certain sense of *déjà vu*. I'd saved her life here then, and come hell or high water, I would save her again.

How the djinn knew about this place, I didn't know. But I was going to find out. It was way too much of a coincidence that he just happened to "find" it. No. Someone here was helping him. I was sure of it.

It didn't escape me that I was taking a great risk with my own life while trying to help Kenya. Although just from what I'd learned about the djinn in this short amount of time, I seriously doubted it would come to that. The djinn was desperate to have someone on his side, to have some semblance of a family that consisted of others like him. And if what he'd told me was true, I was all he had. The odds were pretty low he'd come all this way and had done everything he had to convince me to give him a chance, only to take me out in a fit of temper.

But still...I probably shouldn't fuck this up.

I schooled my thoughts before he decided to take a peek into my head, emptying my brain of everything except what he was telling Kenya. Getting a grip on my emotional reaction to what I was witnessing, however, wasn't so easily done.

Kenya was terrified, and that pissed me right the fuck off. I could see it in the tense way she held her body. In the way her eyes darted around the room. And even how she forgot to behave as though she were human. Her movements were too quick when she made them. And when she didn't, she sat completely still, like a statue, for long periods of time. Her fangs were extended, bared to our view by her lifted upper lip, and every once in a while, a low growl would sound deep in her throat. Like a cornered animal.

I couldn't take my eyes off of her. And it took everything I had in me to stand there so casually and not grab her and run. But I didn't, because I knew damn well we wouldn't even make it out of the house.

No. I needed to bide my time and wait for the right opportunity. Until then, I would be here to make sure nothing happened to her.

Forcing myself to pay attention, I tried to grasp what the djinn was going on about. The story he was weaving was hard to believe. She'd never shown any signs of having any type of magic in her blood—whether it be voodoo or anything else. At least, not that I'd ever seen or felt.

But according to my...uncle—gods, I could barely say the word, even to myself—Kenya was a descendent of the great Marie Laveau herself. "How the hell would you know this?" I asked him.

He gave me a look, letting me know he wasn't happy with the interruption. "This isn't my first run-in with voodoo," he said. "I can taste it in her blood."

Kenya eyes widened behind the lenses of her glasses. "When did you take my blood?"

Marcus heaved a great sigh, like our questions were stretching the limits of his patience. "I didn't take your blood. You left it for me. On the handle of the door to your club."

At first, she looked confused, but then her expression cleared. "My finger. I cut it on the metal plate of the lock that night."

"Yes. That." He looked back and forth between the two of us. "May I continue?" Without waiting for us to answer, he went on. "As I was saying, you have voodoo in your blood, vampire. Not a lot, but enough to give me what I want. I have the bones. I have the spell. You just need to learn how to do it." He looked over at me. "And this is where you come in, Alex."

Well, I wasn't expecting *that*. "Me? I don't know anything about voodoo." The magic that I had in me, dark or not, was an entirely different thing than voodoo.

"No, but you know about magic. You know about spells. How to feel it and how to make it do what you want it to. And you'll only become more and more powerful once I start working with you. And," he continued, "you've lived with voodoo your entire life. You're probably more familiar with it than I am." Leaning back in his chair, he crossed his legs at the knee and laced his fingers on his lap. "So that is how it will work. Once we get back to my mountain, I will teach you to harness the djinn magic in you, while you, Alex, will teach the vampire her voodoo."

"Why me and not you?" I snapped my mouth shut as soon as the words were out of my mouth, wishing I could take them back. Fuck me and my big fucking mouth. I *was* curious why he would give us so much time together, and it wasn't like I wasn't grateful for it, but I also didn't want to give him any reason to spend any more time around her than he already was.

"I will work with her when she is ready. *If* she is ready. Until then, it would only be a waste of my time and energy to try to get something out of her she may not be capable of giving. My own magic is quite different from yours. Also, I have no idea if her vampirism enhanced her abilities or burned them out. But she is all I have, so let's hope it doesn't come to that."

I didn't miss the implied threat there.

"Plus," he smiled, "it will remind you what you are fighting for and give you the chance to become closer to her."

"I really wish you both would stop talking about me like I wasn't sitting right here," Kenya said.

I looked at her, an apology on the tip of my tongue, but stopped myself before I could say it this time. Instead, I ignored her. I could feel the djinn in my head, pressing through the shields I had up like they weren't even there. I didn't want to give him any reason to think I wasn't playing along with his games. But I couldn't help but force his hand on this one thing. "And if she doesn't rise to the challenge?"

He looked down at his lap for a moment. "Then I will have no need for her."

"And she will be mine, as you promised." It came out as half question/half order.

Marcus narrowed his eyes at me. I got the feeling he didn't like me offering up the terms of our agreement in front of Kenya for some reason. "I gave you my word."

Why did I have a feeling his word meant absolute shit?

"Yours?" Kenya asked me. "What the hell is that supposed to mean? I don't want to be yours, or anyone's."

I walked over to where she sat and leaned over her, pressing my palms on the table so we were eye to eye. "You have no say in it. I want you, Kenya. You've known this for a while now. My uncle here needs you to do this thing for him, but when he's through with you, you will come live with me."

She looked up at me, her eyes hard. "No. I won't."

The smile I gave her in return just before I straightened to my full height was an exact replica of the one that so often crossed the djinn's face. I could feel it, and it disgusted me. But I had a part to play, and in order to get us both out of there alive, I had to play it well.

The sooner I got Marcus to trust me, the sooner I would get the chance I was looking for.

But as the djinn glanced at the clock ticking on the wall above us and got up from the table, I knew I was an idiot to hope that chance would come. "I have to leave you two for a little while. There is someone I need to go see."

"Who?" Fear for my sister and the rest of my coven made me forget for a moment who it was I was talking to, and the question shot out before I could stop it. But to my surprise, he answered me.

"There's a certain witch I need to pay a visit to."

My breath froze in my lungs. "*What* witch?"

"Now, that is something you really don't need to know, my nephew. But rest assured, no one will be harmed tonight." He started to walk out of the room but stopped in the doorway. "I do believe this doesn't even need to be said, but the both of you need to stay here. And in case you get any ideas to do otherwise, remember the place is warded. The vampire is bound to this house and the surrounding property."

He didn't need to say anything else. He knew damn well I wouldn't leave her here alone again, no matter how I tried to play it off otherwise. "Yeah. Got it."

"Good."

Once the djinn was gone, I exhaled, some—but not all—of the tension leaving my body. We were still being watched. I looked at Kenya, still sitting exactly where he'd left her. "Is there anything you need?"

She startled at the sound of my voice, her eyes catching mine for a moment before they dropped to the pulse in my throat and quickly darted away. "No."

A rush of desire hit me hard as I imagined her sitting on my lap, her legs on either side of mine and her fangs deep in the side of my throat. I wasn't afraid of a little pain because I had a feeling the pleasure that would come after would make it all completely worth it. "Kenya..." I stared at her, whatever I'd been about to say twisting on my tongue as she stood up and crossed the space between us faster than I could track, appearing in front of me with a challenge in her eyes. So close I could smell the sweet scent of her skin and the coconut in her hair.

"Why are you doing this, Alex?"

I steeled my spine. "Because he's my family."

"You have a family. Here. In New Orleans."

"It's not the same."

"No, it's not," she agreed. Crossing her arms over her chest, she said, "They actually care about you."

I wasn't about to try to argue that point. "But they can't teach me what I need to learn."

"And what is that, Alex? How to be a monster?"

I recoiled as she threw my own words back in my face. Then I shook my head. "No. How to control the darkness inside of me I had to tap into the night I saved you."

She took a step back, looking at me over the rim of her glasses. "So, this is my fault? Is that what you're trying to tell me?"

"No. It's just a fact."

She was silent a moment. And then she asked, "So, would you really stop me if I tried to run from this house right now?"

"No." Because I knew the djinn wouldn't lie about something like that. "I won't have to. You won't get anywhere."

"Why are you being such a bastard?" she whispered.

I wasn't. I was protecting her. I was saving her life, the life of my sister, the lives of my coven. But I couldn't tell her any of that. I didn't know if the djinn was listening. Didn't know if he'd truly left or if he was just testing me.

The latter seemed like the more likely choice. So, I had to play my part.

Turning away from her, I walked out of the room, saying over my shoulder, "Try to run if you'd like. I'll be in here when you get back." Then I went into the living room and sat on the couch, reaching into my pocket for my cell phone. A split second later, Kenya flew past me and bolted out the front door. I leaned back against the cushions and settled in to wait.

She was back sooner than I thought. I'd just swiped open my screen and pulled up Judy's number to let her know we were both okay and not to send anyone looking for us—something I'd debated doing but decided was worth the risk—when I was suddenly knocked off the couch and thrown across the room. I stopped on the other side when I hit the wall, my feet a foot off the floor and Kenya's hand around my throat holding me there. "Let me go!" she screamed in my face.

Anger surged within me and I pushed her away with a wave of my hands. She stumbled back, and I heard a crunch as she stepped on my phone. It had fallen from my fingers when she yanked me from the couch.

I had no time to let that sink in when she was on me again, all fangs and claws and rage, knocking me to the floor. I ended up on my back with her on top of me, her hands holding my arms on either side of my head and her mouth dangerously close to my throat.

"Let me go," she growled. "Or I'll rip out your throat right now."

"No, you won't," I told her quietly. "Because you want me, too." These last words I whispered so quietly no one could possibly have heard me. No one except a vampire.

20

KENYA

Gradually, I eased my grip and released his wrists. The next second, I was off of him and standing across the room by the window, his words ringing in my ears and the scent of his blood too tempting, especially when I was in this agitated state.

Alex got to his feet, his eyes flashing a warning when I bared my fangs at him.

Suddenly, he cocked his head to the side as though he were listening to something. The lights went off and I frowned. Slowly, he raised one finger to his lips.

I became still and waited, feeling the air around me and wondering if the djinn had returned already.

There. Footsteps outside. It sounded like they were coming up along the side of the house, and they didn't belong to the djinn.

Before I could take a step or call out, Alex muttered something under his breath and threw his arms out in an arc, palms toward the front of the house and fingers spread wide. Then he grabbed me and dragged me down to the floor between the couch and the wall, settling me between his legs and slamming his hand over my mouth.

"Not one sound," he growled low in my ear. "Do you understand?"

Oh, I understood all right.

I sank my fangs into the meat of his palm between his thumb and his forefinger. Drops of blood teased my tongue, dark and sweet, and I moaned, my eyes rolling back into my head. Gods, he tasted better than anything I could have imagined.

His answering moan in my ear was the hottest thing I'd ever heard. Masculine. Erotic.

Everything left my mind except the taste of that blood. The footsteps. The reason we were here. I didn't care about any of it. I only cared about tasting more of him.

MINE.

The word roared through my head and made me catch my breath, but only for a moment before I released his hand, only to grab a hold of his arm and pull his wrist over to my lips. I tasted his skin tentatively with the tip of my tongue, the scent of his blood teasing my nose.

"Do it," he ordered in my ear.

I struck, sinking my fangs deep. Ah, gods. I'd never had anything like the blood of this male. He tasted like sin itself, and I wanted to rub his blood all over his naked body and lick it off of him.

"Yes, Kenya." His words were little more than a whisper. "Take me." His other arm wrapped tighter around my waist and pulled me back between his legs until I felt his hard length against my ass.

Through the fog of my bloodlust, I heard someone creeping across the front porch, just on the other side of the wall from where we sat. Fangs deep in his wrist, I stopped sucking, but didn't remove them. Like a voice yelling through a storm, I heard someone call my name. A voice I recognized. But I couldn't think through the bloodlust.

"Please, Kenya. Don't do it."

I only felt his breath on my ear, but I heard his words in my head.

"Do you feel what you do to me?"

Again, the words weren't spoken aloud. Alex was in my head. Or I was in his.

"I want to touch you."

I couldn't stop the sound of need I made then. Pulling my fangs from his wrist, I ran my tongue over the wounds and then made a new bite, letting his dark essence flow freely into my mouth. With my free hand, I moved his other arm down, guiding Alex's fingers to where I wanted them as I let my knees fall to the side, opening myself to his touch.

I knew I shouldn't be doing this. I knew I should be trying to get away, trying to let whoever was outside know I was there.

But I couldn't stop myself.

He caught on right away and wasted no time undoing the fastening of my slacks and sliding his hand inside. His breath caught when he found me, slick and swollen for him.

I drank from him as he touched me, my entire body trembling with need. His fingers teased my clit, then slid inside of me, his hips simulating the movement, only to come back to that bundle of nerve endings.

The muscles low in my groin tightened and released with every surge of desire he pulled from me. His blood roared through my body, sensitizing my skin and igniting my cells. I felt alive. In tune with everything around me. I felt if I opened my eyes, I would hear colors and see sounds.

His breathing quieted in my ear for a moment, and I heard the footsteps stop outside the door. The knob rattled and then stopped, before the steps continued on down off the porch and around the other side of the house.

"Come for me."

His voice, husky and deep and raw with need, reverberated through me, raising goose bumps on my skin. I hovered on the edge of my orgasm, each wave stronger than the last...

"Come for me, Kenya," he ordered.

I crashed over the edge, his wrist tight to my mouth, muting the sounds I made as my orgasm rocked through me, my head thrown back against his shoulder and my fingers digging into his thighs.

"Jesus *Christ*." This time the words were whispered in my ear. "I need to fuck you." He left his hand cupping my cunt possessively as he drew his long legs in, trapping me between them. His hips rocked into me, and I could feel him, thick and hard, straining against his jeans. "Kenya." My name was a plea on his lips.

When my heartbeat slowed and I'd caught my breath enough to think somewhat clearly, I released his wrist, licking the wounds closed. I was exhausted, and yet at the same time I'd never felt more alive. More free. My senses were on high alert. I could hear insects crawling through the marsh outside. The flick of an alligator's tail in the water a mile away. Footsteps growing farther and farther away, not making any effort to stay quiet now. I could see the smallest dust motes floating through the air, reflected in the moonlight coming through a tiny crack in the wall. I was completely satiated.

And yet, I wanted more.

Because all I could smell was Alex. His skin. His blood. His sex. All I could feel was his strength surrounding me. Could hear his blood rushing through his veins and his heart pounding in his chest.

Leaning back against him, I lifted my ass off the floor and slid my slacks down over my hips and off of one leg. As I did that, Alex freed himself from his jeans, his breathing harsh.

In the next second, I was back in his lap and he was sliding inside of me.

He held me there for a second, his fingers digging into my hips. And then he drew his knees up on either side of me, bracing himself, and began to lift me up and down, fucking me as he said he wanted to do. There was nothing sweet about it, just pure animalistic need, and that was just fine with me.

And when that wasn't enough, he slid down the wall until he was flat on his back on the floor and I could get my knees under me. He was deeper now, filling me completely, guiding me with his hands on my hips, his heels digging into the floor. His breathing was loud, harsh, and interspersed with the sexiest sounds.

I wished I could see his face.

He quickened the pace, angling my body to get impossibly deeper. I cried out, all thoughts leaving my head as I found myself with my fingers.

"Kenya...gods..."

My head fell back on my shoulders as my inner muscles clenched tight, the pleasure nearly too much to stand, building up and sending me higher and higher until it was too much and I came crashing down the other side.

With a hoarse cry, he pulled me down hard, and I felt him pulsing inside of me as he found his own release, his breath on the back of my neck as he sat up and pulled me hard against his chest.

We sat this way for a long time. Neither one moving nor saying a word. Afraid to break the spell and go back to the reality of why we were here to begin with.

"Was that Jamal?" I finally asked. "Or Killian?"

"Jamal," he said quietly. "I did a cloaking spell. He wouldn't have seen us even if he'd walked in."

"But he would've heard me?"

"Possibly."

And because Jamal didn't like being in other's heads, he probably never even thought to reach out that way. Of course, I was kind of glad he didn't, because of what he would've heard. "I need to go clean up," I said. Not waiting for permission, I put one hand on the arm of the couch and lifted myself off of his lap, wincing as Alex slid out of me.

His hands gripped my thighs and he dropped a kiss on my bare ass just before I yanked up my slacks and stepped over his legs, heading for the bathroom.

I held it together until I got inside and shut the door behind me. A little bit numb, I kept my mind empty as I opened the door to the small linen closet and found a towel, then I turned on the shower, half expecting the water not to work. But it did. Even the hot water.

With jerky movements, I set my glasses on the sink, removed my shoes and clothes, and left them on the floor as I stepped inside, not caring if my hair got wet.

It was only then, as the warm water ran down my face and body, that I let the tears come. My thoughts too chaotic to release the myriad of emotions inside of me any other way.

But one thing did break through and kept repeating itself over and over.

Mine? How could he be mine?

What gods would play such a cruel joke as to bind me forever to a male who, despite his attraction to me, couldn't care less if I lived or died? And the worst part? I was bound to him now that I'd had his blood. I wouldn't be able to survive without him. Drinking from other humans or from bagged blood, if I could choke it down, would only extend my suffering.

I was already craving Alex again. For blood and for sex.

I don't know how long I'd been standing there when I heard the door open, then the rustling of clothes. The curtain pulled back and I stiffened as Alex got in behind me. With his hands on my arms, he turned me around, slid one hand up to cup my face and lifted my chin until I had no choice but to look at him.

In his dark eyes, I saw none of the chaos I was feeling. "Don't cry," he told me. "Please don't cry."

I made no effort to stem the tears still running down my cheeks. I even sniffed loudly for good measure. "What do you care?"

He caught his bottom lip between his teeth, his eyes full of indecision as they roamed my face. I had to give him credit. He hadn't looked at my boobs once yet.

Finally, he settled, and I could tell by the set of his jaw a decision had been made. "I need to ask you to do something, Kenya."

I sniffed again, and waited.

"I need to ask you to trust me."

I couldn't help it. I laughed out loud through my tears. "Trust you? In what world would you ever think that was possible?"

"I won't hand you over to him."

"Isn't that exactly what you're doing?"

"It's not what you're thinking."

"But you plan to go back with him, don't you?" The djinn was his family. And family was what mattered above all else. This was something I understood, even if I didn't agree with what he was doing. If I had the chance to build a relationship with my blood relatives, I would do it.

He didn't respond to my question, but he didn't have to. I could see the answer in his eyes. And that meant only one thing. I would have to go with him, or I would die the true death.

"Kenya..." He trailed off, for once at a loss for words, and dropped his arms down to his sides.

The steam rose around us, trapping us in our own little reality far away from the cruelty of the real world.

"Is it true?" His eyes roamed over me again, this time dropping down my body, lingering on my breasts and the tight curls between my legs. When they came back to mine, there was fire in his gaze. "That I'm yours?"

21

ALEX

MINE.

It had slammed through my head when Kenya was drinking from me. At first, I thought it was the djinn trying to claim my female. And then I realized it wasn't his inner voice I heard, but Kenya's.

However, it was more than just a word. It was a feeling. An instinct. I felt her possessiveness, her hunger, and it drove me so mad with lust I didn't give a fuck if Marcus was listening to us somehow. Didn't care if Jamal had walked in while I was inside of her. I couldn't have denied her if we'd been dead smack in the center of Bourbon Street in the middle of Mardi Gras.

As she stood before me beneath the shower head, her dark skin wet and glistening, she could've been a goddess of old. Proud.

Mesmerizing. Seductive...and dangerous. My blood roared through my veins and my cock stirred between my legs at the sight of her. "Is it true?"

We really shouldn't be having this conversation. Not here. Not now. But I needed to know, because if this was true, it would explain so much to me.

Still, she wouldn't answer. She just stared at me, her eyes full of remorse.

"Don't look at me like that," I pleaded.

"How am I supposed to look at you?" she finally responded in a thick voice. As soon as she asked the question, she dropped her chin, and when she looked up again there were tears on her cheeks.

Fuck.

I reached for her, wanting to hold her in my arms and tell her it was all right, but she slapped my hands away. "Don't touch me," she spat. "I want nothing to do with you."

"Now we both know that's not true," I told her. And I didn't need to see the way she averted her eyes to know I was right. I wasn't trying to be cocky. I was just trying to be real. "I can feel you, Kenya. I feel your hunger for me. For my blood. And I want to give it to you." My body was hard. Ready. "I want to give it all to you." My life. My heart. My soul. Everything.

She shook her head. "I can't."

"Honey—"

Her eyes threw daggers at me. "Don't you fucking 'honey' me, Alex! Don't you do it!"

I threw my hands in the air, palms out. "Okay. All right." I kept my voice low and calm.

She turned her back to me and stuck her face in the water, wiping away her tears, and I gave her a minute to gather herself while I thought about this new situation. I knew what it meant to be mated to a vampire. She'd fed from me, and now she could *only* feed from me. But for the bond to be completed, I would need to have her blood as well. If not, I would continue to age, and eventually die.

And so would she.

I had to admit, the whole immortality thing was kind of crazy to think about. But I had more important things that needed my immediate attention. Like getting us both out of here alive. But first, I had to let her know I wasn't the monster she thought I was. I was taking a huge chance, talking to her like this. Because if the djinn was dipping into my head, we were pretty much fucked anyway after what had just happened. "Kenya, talk to me. Please."

She turned her head so her stunning profile was visible, but she still wouldn't look at me. "Talk to you?" She laughed, the sound harsh and cruel. "You've been playing me all this time, Alex. You practically handed me over to the djinn—"

"That's not true. I thought you were home. You told me you were home." I reached out to touch her bare back, but pulled back at the last minute. "I swear to you, I had no idea he was anywhere in the area. I didn't know you hadn't gone right home like you'd told me."

"So, again, this is my fault?" She grabbed the soap from the little shelf and began to scrub herself, like she was trying to remove the memories of my touch. It hurt, watching her.

"No, that's not what I'm saying."

She spun around so fast she was nothing but a blur one second and facing me the next. "What exactly *are* you saying, Alex?" She practically spit my name at me.

I clenched my jaw, momentarily forgetting where we were. My hands tightened into fists to keep myself from touching her. All I wanted to do was pull her against me and hold her until the tension left both our bodies, until she would hear what I was trying to say without tipping off the djinn. I couldn't feel him probing around in my head, but I didn't want to take the chance. I felt what I felt, and there wasn't much I could do about that. But as long as I continued to play the part he'd cast me in, it should be okay.

I put everything I was feeling into my eyes, hoping she could read what I was trying to tell her, even without her glasses. "I'm not a monster." Taking a chance, I stepped in closer, lowering my mouth to her ear.

She stiffened, but otherwise didn't move.

"I won't let him harm you. I swear it. I'm asking you to trust me." I straightened just enough that she could see my face, ignoring the spray of water. "I'm asking you," I repeated.

"But how would you stop him?" she asked in a small voice.

My heart shattered into a thousand pieces hearing the fear in her voice. But she was right. My powers were nothing compared to his. Tentatively, I brushed her smooth cheek with the back of my fingers and took a chance. "I don't know, but I will."

She studied me for long moments, and I could see the indecision on her face, the fleeting expressions of hope and anger and fear and longing.

Gods, I wanted to kiss her. I wanted to pull her into my arms and feel all of that smooth, wet skin against mine. And yes, I wanted to fuck her again. It was torture standing so close to her and feeling like she was still so far away.

Finally, she spoke. "You want me to trust you."

I nodded. Gently, I took her face between my hands, giving her plenty of time to pull away.

She didn't.

The kiss was just a brush of my lips to hers, and I felt her bottom lip tremble. "Don't cry," I whispered against her mouth. "Please don't cry. It'll be okay." I wanted to tell her straight out that I was only playing a role. That he would never get us out of this city if I could help it, but that I had to be so careful. There were other lives at stake beside our own.

Kenya wrapped her hands around my wrists, holding my hands to her face as she met my eyes. "It is true," she whispered. "Gods help me, but it is."

Touching my forehead to hers, I closed my eyes and exhaled. "I knew you were mine the moment I saw you dying on that bed weeks ago," I admitted. "I felt it all the way to my bones, and I had to save you. I had to. Because if I didn't, my life would be over." I kissed her head, her nose, her mouth. "Thank you."

"For what?" she asked. "I still think you're a bastard."

"I probably am," I said. "But not in the way you think."

There were questions in her eyes. Things I couldn't answer. At least, not right now. But I could show her how I felt and how much she meant to me. "Let me take care of you," I told her quietly.

"I don't know how to be with someone like you," she whispered.

"I know." Sliding one hand over her shoulder and down her arm, I lifted her hand to my chest. "Touch me," I whispered. "It's okay." I kissed her. Once. Twice. Again. Groaning when I felt the tip of her tongue tasting me. One hand around the back of her neck, I wrapped my other arm around her waist, pulling her against me. My knees went weak when I felt her bare curves against me, and my body hardened even more.

Steam from the hot water rose around us, encompassing us in our own little world as I worshiped her with my hands and mouth until all of the stiffness left her and she was trembling in my arms. Then I lifted her, her legs wrapping around my hips as I pressed her up against the cool tiles and found her entrance with the tip of my cock.

Kenya moaned and rolled her hips against me, her parted lips showing the white tips of her fangs, long and sharp.

I kissed her as I slid inside, feeling her body stretch to accommodate me. She was so tight like this. I gave her a few seconds to make sure she was okay, but when I felt her thighs tighten around me as she tried to lift herself, I cupped her ass and began to move.

Her fingers dug into my back, and she cried out as I thrust into her, fast and hard. It wasn't long before I felt my balls tighten, my orgasm sliding down my spine and up the length of my cock. I slowed down and tilted my head away, exposing my throat. "Feed, Kenya," I rasped.

The sharp tips of her fangs scraped the skin above my jugular and I groaned. "Yes, honey," I told her. "It's okay. Do it."

Fast as a viper, she struck, her fangs sliding through my skin to sink into my vein. I cried out, the feel of her fangs in me and my cock in her pussy too much. My orgasm hit me like a truck, roaring through me as I thrust into her even deeper, my hips jerking uncontrollably.

Kenya moaned against my throat, her body tightening on my sex momentarily before she convulsed around me, taking everything I had.

And when it was done and she'd pulled her fangs from my throat, I sank to my knees with her still on my lap, too lightheaded to stay upright. The water hitting my back was cooling off. I guess we'd hit our limit on shower time.

"Alex?" Kenya's hands were on me, pulling my head from her shoulder so she could look at me. "Alex, are you okay?"

"I'm fine." I smiled at her.

But she shook her head. "No. No. Shit. I took too much."

Wrapping my fingers around her wrists, I pulled her hands away, kissing the inside of each wrist before I held them between us. "Seriously, I'm okay. I just..." There were no words to describe what I'd just gone through. "If I'd only known how that felt, I would've insisted on feeding you that first night we kissed."

I'd meant it to be a joke, but she didn't laugh. Didn't even crack a smile. "Are you sure you're okay?"

I kissed her softly. "I am. And Kenya?"

"Hmm?"

"Be ready," I told her. I held her eyes, hoping I got my meaning across.

Her eyebrows lowered, those cute little creases appearing between them. Then suddenly, her expression cleared, and her fingers tightened around mine. She nodded.

I kissed her again and helped her to her feet as I got to mine. I was still a bit woozy, but overall, not too bad. At least I was able to stay upright now. We rinsed off and I turned off the water, now quite cool. Then we got out, dried off and got dressed.

Neither one of us said a word the entire time. As though we both knew now that we'd left what little protection the shower provided, we had to be extremely careful.

But I was getting her out of here. Tonight. The barrier the djinn had around the property should be nothing but a simple binding spell. Even if it was something stronger, I should be able to open it enough for her to slip out. Then I would follow her. Once we were out, we just had to get to the city and the help of my coven.

Surely, between all of us, we'd be able to fend off the djinn.

Right?

22

KENYA

"Run."

Chills ran down my spine as Alex's breath tickled my ear. We'd been standing in the living room when he'd suddenly walked up behind me. We'd been waiting for the last hour, both of us quiet since the "shower scene" that I was still trying to process.

I frowned, sure I hadn't heard him right. But when I looked at Alex, I saw the truth staring back at me. He was letting me go. "What about the spell? I can't leave. I already tried."

"I can lower it just long enough for you to get out, but you need to run faster than you've ever run in your life. I won't be able to hold it long."

Immediately, I shook my head. "Not without you." I couldn't leave him here to face Marcus's wrath alone. He wouldn't survive it. I knew this all the way to my bones. And although the thought of seeing him again in a different life—one that had no djinn in it—was enough to bring a smile to my face, I wasn't yet done living this one. And neither was he. For the sake of the gods, I'd just found him. And although I didn't know how to love him, the thought of losing him was an unbearable agony that had nothing to do with the blood bond.

He clenched his jaw, his voice low but urgent. "Jesus Christ, Kenya. Fucking run! Now!"

I held my ground. "No. Not without you."

At first, I thought he was going to yell at me some more, but then his expression softened. "I'll meet you back in the city. At the club," he added. "But I can't do what I need to do to get out of this alive with you here. Now fucking RUN."

He shoved me forward as the sound of a car engine drew closer. My heart in my throat with fear for him, I did as he told me to do, running toward the back of the house where the walls were caving in. Knocking a board loose, I jumped through and ran, losing myself in the trees surrounding the house. I didn't stop and I didn't look back. Not even when I heard Marcus scream with rage and a sound like the house was caving in on itself. Not even when I came up to the place where the djinn's spell should stop me. Lowering my chin, I pumped my arms and legs...

And burst through with only the slightest resistance.

Tears overflowed, blurring my vision, and still I ran. I had no idea where I was going, and it wasn't until I plunged into the waist deep waters of the swamp and got smacked in the face by a Bald Cypress branch that I realized I'd gone in a circle. I stopped, my heart pounding in my ears. There was a splash to my right, and something brushed past my left thigh. Vegetation maybe. Or a snake.

Suddenly, the air pressure changed, ebbing and flowing in a weird wave of magic. I had no time to react before a second wave, this one much stronger than the first, hit me from behind, throwing me forward and knocking me face down into the cold water. I scrambled to my feet, the water now up to my chest, and backtracked the way I had come as fast as I could go.

When I found solid ground, I stopped for a second, getting my bearings, but I couldn't bring myself to move again, to leave him.

I wouldn't leave him.

If Alex could distract him long enough, I could sneak up behind him and twist off his head. The thought made me shudder. I hadn't been a violent human, and I was even less so as a vampire, always relying on everyone around me to save me.

Well, tonight, I was the one who was going to do the saving.

Mind made up, I took a deep breath, bracing myself for what I needed to do, then I ran back the way I'd come, ignoring the fear that wound its way through me, threatening to freeze my limbs and send me flying onto my face again. Dodging trees and brush when I could and crashing through them when I couldn't, I ran.

As I got closer, I was more careful of my path, not wanting to alert Marcus with all the noise. Slowing to a jog, I wiped the moisture from my cheeks from tears that refused to stop falling and tried to slow my racing heart. Once I was inside the border, I wouldn't be able to leave again until the djinn was dead.

Suddenly, a female appeared in front of me. I skidded to a halt, wondering where the hell she had come from. She was quite lovely, with pale skin, long, dark hair and green eyes that shone even in the darkness. Immediately sensing she was a vampire, I instinctively crouched into a fighting stance and bared my fangs in warning. This was not her territory. Which only told me she was here to cause trouble I didn't fucking need right now.

She held her hands out in front of her, palms toward me. "Whoa, there."

I noticed she kept her voice down. I also noticed she wasn't distracted by the noise coming from the swamp house. "Who the hell are you?" I asked her. Then I shook my head. "I don't have time for this."

"Please," she said. "My name is Shea. And this,"—without taking her eyes from me, she tilted her head to the side where a man in a black robe appeared—"this is my mate. His name is Jesse. And we're not here to hurt you."

Slowly, I straightened as the fear I'd tried to hold at bay broke through the dam and flooded through me, making my teeth chatter and my muscles tremble. I didn't know who the hell these two were, but I did know djinn magic when I felt it now, and the guy with her was oozing with it.

Something rustled over our heads, and a large raven swooped down through the branches of a tree, landing on the man's shoulder. She made clicking noises at him, rubbing her beak on his cheek, before turning one black, beady eye toward me.

"This is Cruthú," the female told me. "She's here to help also. And there's a few more of us." She lifted her chin in the direction of the road. "They're waiting for my call before they come in."

"Who the hell *are* you?" I asked again, though my eyes never left the male with the large bird on his shoulder.

"Please," the female said. "We don't have much time. Your male won't hold out much longer. We need to help him."

"Why would you help him?" I demanded.

"Because I don't want him to accidentally kill my father," the male said in a low voice. "That honor is reserved for me, and me alone."

My eyes flew to the female and she gave me a tentative smile.

"I still don't understand—" I was cut off by a scream of pain coming from the direction of the house. "Alex!" I called, not caring anymore if Marcus knew I was still there. I went to run past the female, but her hand whipped out and she grabbed my arm, holding me there.

"Go," she told the male. "And be careful," she demanded.

His lips curved up at the corners, but there was nothing at all pleasant about it. I shivered as he stepped closer to us. He glanced at me, his eyes glowing a bright yellow, then he dropped a hard kiss on her lips and said, "I'll be right back, love."

I watched as he left us, walking swiftly toward the house, his robe billowing out behind him and the raven on his shoulder.

Once he was gone, the female—Shea—released my arm. "I'm sorry I grabbed you like that. But please don't run off," she said. "You'll only be a distraction, and that distraction may cause my mate his life. And then I would have to kill you, and I'd really rather we be friends."

I turned hard eyes on her. "Will he save Alex?"

"Yes," she told me with confidence. "If you stay here and let him do it."

"Do I have a choice?"

She smiled sweetly. "Nope."

Adrenaline still rushed through my body, and I shifted my weight from one side to the other, finding it hard to settle in and wait.

"What's your name?" she asked me.

"Kenya."

"Killian is your master, right? Irish guy? Pale? Powerful?"

Glancing at her, I nodded.

"Does he know where you are?"

I shook my head. "No."

"Well, he will soon."

I shoved my hair off my face, watching in the direction of the house. It was quiet. Eerily so. I wished she would just shut up.

As if she'd read my thoughts—which she may well have—Shea said, "I know you wish I'd just shut my face, but I'm talking as much to keep myself distracted as you." Quietly, she added, "That's the love of my life in there. He's scary. And he's not who I imagined myself with, but he's mine. And I would be completely lost without him. So, I need to talk to you to keep myself from rushing in there. I swore to him I wouldn't, and it's the only reason he allowed me to come. Plus," she smiled. "I told him he needed me here to keep you out of the way when we found out what was going on."

"How did you find out where we were?"

"Witches," she told me. "Apparently, there's some sort of a spell hiding you guys so when they tried to do a location spell, it wouldn't work. However, we brought a secret weapon."

When she didn't continue, I raised my eyebrows and waited.

"Keira Moss," she said. "She knew how to get around it."

"How did she do that?" Then I waved my hand in the air and shook my head. "No. Know what? I don't even care."

But she answered me anyway. "She's a powerful witch. It totally freaks out Luukas when she uses her magic, though."

"Luukas?"

"Luukas Kreek. Master vampire of the Pacific Northwest. And her mate," she added.

"Why does it freak him out?"

"That's a long story for another time. But let's just say he's been through a lot, so when you meet him, don't let him scare you. He's a good male. Just...he's been through a lot," she repeated.

An orange flash lit up the sky, and I think we both stopped breathing.

23

ALEX

I felt the bones break in my back as I hit the tree. With a grunt of pain I fell to the ground, my face smacking off of one of the exposed roots.

I was going to die here. I knew this now. My own power was nothing at all compared to the djinn's. He threw me around like a rag doll with nothing but a wave of his hand, playing with me, and knocking aside anything I threw at him.

I was fucking exhausted. The only thing that kept me going was the fact that I was giving Kenya time to escape and get to The Purple Fang. Hopefully, the ward I'd put around the building would be enough to keep Marcus out until my coven could figure something out, until it gradually faded away with my death. Maybe they could even figure out a way to keep her alive once I was gone. But I was wondering now if the djinn had only been fucking with us that first night. If my spell would keep him out at all.

In any case, I wasn't going to last much longer. Weakening the binding spell for Kenya had taken more out of me than I'd expected. Maybe she'd been right and the blood loss was a part of it, too. I didn't know. A sense of foreboding filled me. A foreshadowing of my own death. I'd overestimated his need for me. Gotten too puffed up with my own importance to him. Too cocky. The truth of it was he didn't give that much of a shit about anyone. He only cared about what he wanted. His own power. Family or not, he was going to kill me.

I'm so sorry, Kenya.

His boots appeared in front of my eyes. "Get up," he told me. "And go get the vampire. I *need* her." He nudged me with his toe, and I bit back a yelp of pain. Guess my spinal cord was still intact after all, because it hurt like fuck. "Come on, Alex. What kind of warlock are you? Heal yourself, boy. Stop this foolishness and do as I say."

I don't know what he thought I was, but I couldn't heal myself. Only a certain kind of witch was able to heal themselves, and sometimes others if they were particularly strong.

I was not one of those witches.

And even if I were, I wouldn't do it, just to piss him off. Pushing myself slowly and painfully to my side, I waited until he looked me in the eye before I spoke. "Fuck. You." Blood filled my mouth, and I spit it out, aiming for his feet. I managed to splatter one shiny shoe, but not the other.

Good enough.

I watched as his eyes faded completely to black. My head began to ache, the pain increasing until I felt like worms were digging through my brain matter. I clenched my teeth, refusing to give him the satisfaction of hearing my suffering, but I couldn't stop myself from clamping my hands to either side of my head. My eyes bulged, and I closed them tight in an attempt to keep them in their sockets. Clenching my jaw against the scream that welled in my throat, I knew that at any moment my head was going to explode, and there was nothing I could do to stop it.

Something screeched above our heads, and the pressure in my skull let up a fraction as Marcus frowned, looking up into the night sky. Fighting the blackness that threatened to overwhelm me, I tried to see what had distracted him from my death.

A raven, black as the sky above it, circled above our heads.

"Hello, Father."

Marcus whipped around, releasing me from my torture. My head hit the ground as my vision went in and out. I tried to lift it, to see what was happening, but the world moved around me in slow motion, going in and out of focus until I finally lost the battle and my face sank into the wet ground.

Breathing in an out of my mouth, I fought to stay conscious. When I thought I could handle it, I gritted my teeth and pushed with one arm, rolling onto my back. My vision went white, and then black, and then finally cleared.

A creature with glowing yellow eyes in a flowing, black robe stood about twenty feet away, its face hidden by the large hood. As I watched, the raven swooped down, batting Marcus in the face with her wing before landing on the creature's shoulder.

I closed my eyes.

Sweet darkness swallowed me.

When I opened them again, Marcus was talking.

"...son. How did you find..."

His voice went in and out as my eyes slid closed again.

"What do you think you're going to do...you left me!"

And the creature with the glowing eyes...

"Kill you."

The djinn laughed, loud and obnoxious, making my head ache.

The next time I woke, it was to a flash of bright orange light and the scream of the raven. I tried to lift my arm to block my eyes. Red hot pain blazed through my body from my head to my tailbone at even that slight movement.

Darkness descended...

"Alex!"

Kenya.

I tried to say her name, to let her know I was still here, but I don't know if anything came out.

"Get Grace!"

A woman's voice. I didn't recognize it.

Minutes or hours later, I honestly didn't fucking know, cool hands gripped my head.

"What do you think, love?" a man asked in a British accent.

I never heard the reply, or even if there was one.

Something sweet dripped past my lips to my tongue. "Mmm..."

"He's coming around."

It seared my throat like fire, but it didn't burn. No. It was more like the warm rush of a good liquor, and I thought at first that someone was pouring whiskey into my mouth.

But unlike alcohol, this stuff didn't relax me. Just the opposite. I moaned as it spread through my chest, hitting my stomach and rushing out to the very ends of my limbs. Electricity sparked through my back, the bones that had been crushed against the tree adjusting themselves slowly and painfully.

I cried out, my voice raspy and thick with whatever they were giving me.

The pain stopped for a moment, and then something was pressed against my mouth. The flow of fluid was faster this time, and I swallowed a great mouthful as once again hands pressed to the sides of my head.

"Drink, Alex. Come on. Drink for me."

I did as Kenya told me to do, knowing she wouldn't hurt me, and sucking hard when the flow threatened to stop.

White light flashed behind my closed eyes, like fireworks, and I moaned.

"Keep drinking, Alex. Just keep drinking. It's okay. It'll be okay..." Kenya's voice drifted away.

I did as she told me, taking in great mouthfuls of the liquid and doing my best to ignore the pain of my body and the twinges and flashes going on in my head.

A woman spoke behind me, her voice soft, her words unintelligible.

Still, I drank. I drank until the fire filled my blood, until my muscles clenched with need and my cock swelled in my pants. Blindly, I reached for Kenya, one hand finding her waist and the other discovering it was her arm pressed to my mouth.

Her blood I drank.

Ah, *gods*.

I moaned as it filled me, healed me, made me feel like the strongest man alive.

All except my head.

"Keep drinking," she whispered.

"Kenya," the first woman I'd heard spoke again. "He's taking too much."

"It's fine," she told her, but her voice sounded weak. Thready. "He can take whatever he needs."

Was I drinking too much? I tried to slow down, to take it easy, but it was like a heroin addict trying to stop pushing the plunger after only getting a drop. Like an alcoholic trying to put down the bottle after only having one shot.

Gradually, I realized the lights in my head had dimmed, the pain in my body little more than a dull throb.

The hands that were holding my head lifted away.

"Grace? Here, let me help you, love." The British voice again.

"Alex?"

I blinked my eyes open to find Kenya's lovely face above me, her hair blocking the dark sky behind her and her wrist still pressed to my mouth. A tear fell, hitting me on the forehead.

"You need to stop drinking, Alex," the first female voice said. I shifted my eyes slightly to the right to see a pretty woman with pale skin and dark hair. "I know she tastes great and all that, but you're taking too much."

Immediately, I released her arm from my grip. I didn't even realize I was still holding it.

She lifted her wrist to her mouth, licking the wound closed. Now that I could see her clearly, she did look a bit woozy.

I sat up so fast she didn't have time to get out of the way, taking her in my arms. "Take some of it back," I demanded.

But she just shook her head, her soft curls brushing my face. "I'm okay. You need it more than I do right now." Then she wiggled her arms out from between our bodies and wrapped them around my neck, squeezing tight as a deep sob shook her. "I thought I'd lost you," she told me. "I thought he'd killed you."

I held her tight and let her cry. Over her shoulder, I eyed up the crowd that stood around us, including the creature with the glowing yellow eyes.

As I watched, it pushed the hood back off its head, and I saw that it was not a creature at all, but a man. He gave me a nod when he saw me staring at him.

I turned my face into Kenya's neck. "Who are all these people?" I asked her.

"I have no idea," she told me. "But they saved you."

24

KENYA

Killian shook hands with Luukas, the master vampire from Seattle, Washington. Apparently, while Alex and I were trapped at the swamp house, he had called Killian and gotten permission to bring his vampires and their mates into our territory. Once here, the scary one in the black robe—the warlock—had asked that he call the witch coven and invite them to The Purple Fang. Killian had closed the club, and once everyone was there and introduced, the warlock had explained why they'd all made the trip.

The witches had been especially thrilled to find out they had more family just a short plane ride away.

Imagine their surprise when they found out the djinn was not only here, but that he'd taken me, and Alex had gone missing when he'd tried to find me. It didn't help that I'd stepped on his phone.

Jamal had filled them all in with anything they didn't know, and Killian was furious with me for not telling him about Alex's involvement. But I didn't care. All I cared about right now was that the djinn was gone, and Alex and I were both alive and safe.

The scary one, Jesse, was furious Marcus had escaped him. That flash of light Shea and I had seen was a spell thrown by the djinn, one Jesse couldn't track or counter, enabling him to get away. The raven had flown around, covering a good mile radius or more around the swamp house, but when she'd come back, the warlock told us she'd seen nothing. He'd walked away, stroking her feathers and whispering words of assurance that she had done well. I'd never seen such a relationship between a warlock and a bird before.

"You get used to her," Shea had told me. "Although she does hog a lot of his attention."

Now we were all gathered in the kitchen of the house and I'd just finished telling Killian what the djinn had told me about myself. Alex sat next to me at the small kitchen table, holding my hand and refusing to leave my side.

Killian stared down at the table. "When I found you as a human, you'd already bled out so much you were on death's door."

Alex's fingers tightened around mine and I smiled at the look on his face.

"I didn't need to do anything but give you my blood to turn you," Killian continued. "If there's voodoo in you, Kenya, I wouldn't know it. And I don't know that I would be able to tell anyway. I taste nothing in Lizzy's blood that tells me she's a witch. I only know that she appeases my thirst better than any others."

I caught the High Priestess's grimace from the corner of my eye. When she caught me looking at her though, she smiled, and her smile was kind. Then she shrugged. "I can't help it," she said. "Just the thought..."

She made another face and I smiled as Lizzy scolded her.

"Aunt Jude!"

"It's an acquired taste," I told her. "Even I had to get used to it at first."

"I would imagine."

"So, what's next?" Alex asked, directing his question at Jesse.

"That remains to be seen," he told him. "If it's all right with you,"—he looked pointedly at Killian and Judy—"I'd like us to remain here a few more days and see what I can find out."

Killian nodded as Judy said, "Of course."

I looked between the two males. It was obvious they were related, from their dark hair, strong jawlines, and golden eyes, to the dark feel of their magic. The warlock and his mate had arrived just in time to save Alex and I, bringing the other vampires and witches from Seattle with them, and for that I would always be grateful. Killian, Lizzy, and Judy had arrived later, after it was all over.

However, I didn't know that I'd ever be comfortable around him. And from the way everyone else except his mate gave him the side-eye, I wasn't alone in that.

"How about we get you home?" Killian told me. "Yeah?"

"I'll go back with Alex," I told him. "Can you leave us a car?"

Killian narrowed his eyes at me, but then Lizzy touched his arm. "You can have ours. We'll ride back with Aunt Jude."

"Kenya will be coming back with us," Killian said, his tone not allowing for any arguments.

But Lizzy rolled her eyes. "Killian. He saved her life. Again. I don't think there's any danger in letting him give her a ride home."

He looked like he was about to say more, but then he made the mistake of catching his mate's eyes with his. After a moment, he sighed and slid his keys and his cell phone across the table. "Call Lizzy's phone if you need anything. You know the code."

"Yes," I told him. "Thank you."

He got up from the table, ran his eyes over Alex and the way he was still holding my hand, and then he nodded.

A few minutes later, they were all on their way back to the city and we were alone at the table.

"I'm so sorry," Alex told me. His voice broke and he looked down at our hands for a moment, then back at me.

In his eyes, I saw nothing but anguish.

"Sorry? Alex, you saved us."

He made a disgusted noise. "I didn't. I was weak. And I almost killed us both."

"No. You were not."

But he wasn't listening to me. "If I'd just waited a little bit longer, Jesse and Shea would have gotten here, and I could've helped him take out Marcus. But no. I had to be the fucking hero."

I would never understand the male mind. "We didn't know they were coming. I didn't even know they were here until they showed themselves. Jesse must've cloaked himself and Shea somehow. Alex—" I waited until he was looking at me. "You didn't know. And what if they hadn't been here?" I asked him. "You. Saved. Us."

All I got was a grunt of acknowledgment that perhaps I was right. It would have to be good enough. "I really thought you were on his side," I told him softly.

That got his attention. "I know. I'm so sorry." He released my hand just long enough to pull his chair closer to me. Turning me toward him, he pushed my glasses up on the bridge of my nose. "And I should be furious with you for coming back instead of running like I'd told you to."

"I couldn't leave you here alone to fight him, Alex."

"Why not?"

I frowned. "Why not?"

A smile played around the corners of his mouth. "Yes. Why not, Kenya? Why couldn't you leave me?"

249

Heat travelled from my chest to my neck and finally my cheeks. "You know why."

"I do. But I want to hear you say it."

It wasn't an order, more of a plea. And when I looked up at him, I could see the longing in his beautiful eyes, the apprehension.

"Because you're mine," I whispered.

He swallowed hard. "And?"

"And..." My heart began to race, the words getting stuck in my throat.

Alex touched my face, his eyes on mine, holding me there so I couldn't look away as he waited. I thought of Shea and her love for her djinn. And she did love him. Anyone with eyes could see that.

"And I think I'm falling in love with you," I confessed.

Out of all the things I thought I would feel at this moment—fear, nervousness, doubt—relief wasn't one of them. But that was exactly how I felt, relieved to finally tell him. Relieved the others finally knew. Relieved we didn't have to hide anymore. I found myself blinking away tears as my heart filled my chest to the point that I thought it was going to explode.

"That's good," he told me, taking my hands in his and holding them on my lap. "Because I've known from the moment I saw you lying in that bed back there,"—he lifted his chin toward the back of the house—"your hair a tangle of frizzy curls around your gorgeous face and your beautiful skin gray with whatever the hell that disease was Marcus cast on you, that you were meant for me. Maybe even before that, if I'm going to be completely honest. I couldn't take my eyes off you. And the thought of you dying..." He stopped, glancing away as he cleared his throat. "Kenya, I had to save you. I fucking had to."

Something in his voice drew my attention. "You knew," I said. "You knew it would bring out the djinn side of you."

He just looked at me.

"Alex..."

But he shook his head. "I didn't know what it was, exactly, only that it was something dark and unlike any other magic I'd ever known." He looked down at our joined hands, and when his eyes came back to mine, they were full of a stubborn rebelliousness. "I knew what it would do to me, to tap into it. But I couldn't allow you to die. I wasn't going to give you up. Not for a curse. Not for a fucking djinn. You're *mine*, Kenya. And he can't fucking have you."

"Why not?" I threw his own question back at him.

Alex's expression softened. Lifting my hands to his mouth, he kissed the insides of both my wrists one at a time, something that always made butterflies flutter in my stomach, then he leaned in and brushed my lips with his. "Because I'm falling in love with you, too," he whispered against my mouth.

I moaned as he kissed me. His mouth possessive on mine. His magic wrapping around me. Only this time, I wasn't frightened by it.

When he finally broke away from me, he said, "I can't stand to be away from you. But we need to get you home before the sun comes up."

"Come back to the house with me," I told him.

He stood, pulling me up beside him. "Killian won't like that."

"Killian will have to get used to it."

Surprised by the vehemence in my voice, he stopped. "I guess he will."

"Yes, he will. Because I'm hungry for you, Alex."

He growled low in his throat and caught me up against him, his body hard, ready.

I wrapped my arms around his neck and kissed him, not hiding anything from him this time.

"Kenya..." he moaned. "Ah, honey." His arms tightened around me, and then he swooped down and gathered me up into his arms. Striding through the house, he willed the front door open and took me out to the car, all the while telling me all of the dirty things he wanted to do to me as I grazed his throat with my fangs, drops of his blood teasing my tongue.

I think we're going to need to get our own place.

EPILOGUE

ANGEL MOSS

I wrapped one arm around the djinn's waist, propping him up against me. Luckily, I was tall enough and strong enough that his weight didn't send me to the ground. Thank the gods for Krav Maga.

His sorcery fluttered around me, broken and weak. I don't think he was capable of drawing it back.

It gave me hope.

"Don't even think it, witch," Marcus breathed. "I'll be back to normal by the time we reach the city." He grunted as he tripped over something on the ground, his arm tightening around the back of my neck and his fingers digging painfully into my shoulder even through my thick coat. "I was caught by surprise. Otherwise, they would all be dead right now."

I caught a glimmer of water on the ground and redirected us to skirt the edge of the swamp. The urge to toss him in and leave him there to feed the gators wouldn't go away, but somehow, I restrained myself.

"Do not forget our deal, witch."

"Stay the fuck out of my head, djinn," I grumbled. I would keep my end of the stupid agreement I'd made. I had to. I had no other choice. But I didn't have to like it.

"Just get me back to the city," he told me. "And, for now, your part in all this will be over. At least until I need you again."

I stepped over a fallen tree branch, and my boot sank down into the muck. Yanking it out, I moved us further away from the water. Clouds had suddenly filled the night sky, and I couldn't see for shit. "I didn't agree for this to be an on-call arrangement. That wasn't our deal. I told you your niece and nephew were alive and living here. I gave you a hideout where no one would find you—"

"Not so hidden anymore."

"—and I'm helping your ass not get killed by some crazy ass monk and his bird. So, I do believe I've gone above and beyond our original agreement. This was a one-time thing, Marcus."

"I've changed my mind."

He changed his mind.

Tears burned the inside of my eyelids, but I blinked them away. I was an idiot to get involved with all of this. But getting all teary wouldn't change anything. What I needed to do was think.

No. First, I needed to get this bastard the hell away from me and out of my head. I tried to keep him out, but every once in a while my shields would slip and he'd be waiting. He didn't trust me. And I didn't blame him. He shouldn't trust me at all, because as soon as I found a way to get out of this situation I'd put myself in, I would turn on him faster than a viper.

I saw my car up ahead and quickened our pace. Dumping him into the backseat, I jogged around the front of the car and got into the driver's seat. Pushing the ignition button, I left the headlights off for now, praying to any god who would listen that I wouldn't drive us right into the swamp. Luckily, there was plenty of brush here lining the dirt road that led to the house.

By the time we got to the city, Marcus was sitting up in the backseat, his phone in his hand.

"Where should I drop you?" I asked him.

"The airport," he told me.

I glanced in the rearview mirror, taking note of his of ragtag appearance. "You don't think you'll raise a few suspicions walking in there looking like that?"

He looked up from his phone, then swung his arms out to the side as he eyed his clothes. "You're absolutely right." With a wave of his hand, he was dressed in a white dress shirt, a black jacket, and—I would assume—clean, pressed dress slacks. His dark hair was combed back from his face, and there wasn't a speck of grime on him. "That should do it." Then he went back to his phone.

"Who are you talking to?" I asked, hoping my voice didn't betray my anxiety. There was only one reason he should be on his phone right now, and that reason had damned well better be alive and well when I got back to my apartment.

"I'm making arrangements for my flight back to my mountain."

I kept my eyes on the road, but I had to consciously loosen my grip on the steering wheel before he noticed. "Don't you just mind-fuck everyone into doing what you want?"

"To a point," he said, without explaining further.

A few minutes passed by. I turned onto I-10 and headed to the airport. "What about our deal?" I asked him. "You can't just leave him as he is."

I refused to look at him. Wouldn't allow him to see the pleading in my eyes. He was silent for so long I thought he was going to ignore my question.

Finally, he sighed. "He will be released after I get onto the plane and it's in the air." Marcus leaned forward until his mouth was right behind my ear, and I had to repress the urge to shiver with repulsion when I felt his hot breath on my neck. "However," he said quietly. "There is a very strong thread between us now. I can easily find him anywhere and do whatever I please to him. So I would strongly suggest that you don't get any ideas after I leave. You are still held to your end of the deal. And if I call you, you will answer. *That* is the new deal."

"You're a motherfucker," I told him through my teeth.

He chuckled, and leaned back in his seat again. "So I've been told."

I hope you enjoyed Alex and Kenya's story! Keep reading with...

Forsworn by the Vampire

I made a deal with a devil. And now I'm paying for my sins.

But I have a plan to fix it...until a certain vampire gets in my way. Jamal is the epitome of tall, dark, and seductive. And he needs me (and my blood) more than he wants to admit. Too bad he'd literally rather die than be mine. However, I'm not ready to let him go...

I was born a slave. I refused to die as one.

Not even for a witch like Angel Moss. With hair like fire and a body made for sin, nothing about her lived up to her name. That right there should have been enough to warn me away, but like a moth to a flame, I'm lured into her secrets. And with the first taste of her blood, the truth slams into me like a nightmare come true.

Angel is MINE, only she isn't taking me to heaven.

She's dragging me to hell.

Click Here To Read Forsworn by the Vampire

If you haven't read the original Deathless Night story where we first meet Luukas and the rest of the vampires, along with their mates, you can start reading here with **A Vampire Bewitched**.

If you don't want to go all the way back to book one, **Night of the Vampire** is a great entry point as the series picks up the storyline of the Moss witches.

Already read all of Deathless Night and looking for more? The Kincaid Werewolves have their own series, and you can start with **Lone Wolf's Claim**.

Check out my website **HERE** for even more books and the reading order of each series!

Thanks again for reading!

Much love,

L.E.

ABOUT THE AUTHOR

L.E. Wilson writes romance starring intense alpha males and the women who are fearless enough to love them just as they are. In her novels you'll find smoking hot scenes, a touch of suspense, some humor, a bit of gore, and multifaceted characters, all working together to combine her lifelong obsession with the paranormal and her love of romance.

Her writing career came about the usual way: on a dare from her loving husband. Little did she know just one casual suggestion would open a box of worms (or words as the case may be) that would forever change her life.

On a Personal Note:

"I love to hear from my readers! Contact me anytime at le@lewilsonauthor.com."